1

Kate Hardy lives in Norwich, in the east of England, with her husband, two children, one bouncy spaniel, and too many books to count! When she's not busy writing romance or researching local history, she also loves cooking—see if you can spot the recipes sneaked into her books. (They're also on her website, along with excerpts and the stories behind the books.)

Writing for Harlequin Mills & Boon has been a dream come true for Kate—something she wanted to do ever since she was twelve. She's been writing Medical Romances since 2001, and also writes for RIVA; her novel BREAKFAST AT GIOVANNI'S won the Romantic Novelists' Association's Romance Prize in 2008. She says she loves what she does because she gets to learn lots of new things when she's researching the background to a book: add warmth, heart and passion, plus a new gorgeous hero every time, and it's the perfect job!

Kate's always delighted to hear from readers, so do drop in to her website at www.katehardy.com

A MOMENT ON THE LIPS

BY
KATE HARDY

First published in Great Britain 2011
by Mills & Boon, an imprint of Harlequin (UK) Limited,
Eton House, 18-24 Paradise Road, Richmond, Surrey TW9 1SR

© Pamela Brooks 2011

ISBN: 978 0 263 22100 8

Also by Kate Hardy:

RED WINE AND HER SEXY EX
CHAMPAGNE WITH A CELEBRITY
GOOD GIRL OR GOLD DIGGER?
TEMPORARY BOSS, PERMANENT MISTRESS
HOTLY BEDDED, CONVENIENTLY WEDDED

Did you know these are also available as eBooks?
Visit www.millsandboon.co.uk

For Gerard, Chris and Chloe. *Sempre.*

CHAPTER ONE

IT WAS her shoes that gave her away.

Her business suit was fine. Professional. Like her pristine leather briefcase, barely there make-up and the way she wore her long hair in a simple yet elegant twist. But the heels of her shoes were much too high and much too delicate. They weren't office shoes: they were do-me heels. And Dante Romano had known enough princessy types in his time to recognise that these were *expensive* do-me heels. The kind that only a rich, spoiled woman could afford.

Closing this deal was obviously going to be much less time-consuming than he'd feared. So much for his sources telling him that Carenza Tonielli was serious about taking over the family business.

'Thank you for coming to see me, Signorina Tonielli,' he said, standing up. 'May I offer you some coffee? Water?' He indicated the bottle and glasses on his desk.

'Water would be lovely, thank you.'

'Please, have a seat.' He gestured to the chair on the far side of his desk and waited until she'd sat down before pouring them both a glass of water and sitting down again himself.

She picked up her glass and took a sip of water.

Beautiful hands, he thought. And shook himself mentally as a picture flashed through his head. Oh, for pity's sake. Yes, Carenza Tonielli was beautiful. Probably the most beautiful woman he'd ever met. But she was also very aware of it, and he wasn't interested in doing anything other than business with a spoiled princess.

Liar, his libido corrected. *You were thinking about what those hands would feel like against your skin. And that mouth.*

That beautiful mouth. A perfect rosebud. Well, he might be thinking about it, but he certainly wasn't going to act on his thoughts. He didn't have the time. Not if he was going to hit the targets for his business plan. Until the franchise was off the ground, his social life was taking a definite back seat. And he wasn't about to indulge his libido.

'So why did you want to see me?' she asked.

Was she really that clueless? Poor Gino. He'd made a huge mistake, handing over the business to his wayward granddaughter in the hope that she'd come good. The girl who'd left Naples to party her way round the world—and it had taken her ten years to come home. Was she really going to exchange *la dolce vita* for one of sheer hard work to turn the business around?

From what his sources in London had said, Dante was pretty sure that all Carenza Tonielli was interested in was having enough money to buy herself a new designer outfit for every party she attended, drink the very best champagne, and drive the very latest sports car.

None of which she'd be able to do, given the state Tonielli's was in right now.

Well, he wouldn't cheat her. He'd give her a fair price, the same as he'd offered her grandfather. She'd get the cash she needed to finance her lifestyle, and he'd get a brand name that would help make his business grow. It was the perfect win-win situation for both of them. And hopefully she'd see that, too.

'I was negotiating a deal with your grandfather. To buy out Tonielli's,' he said.

'Oh.'

'So, since he's handed the reins over to you, I assume that you're the one I need to negotiate with now.'

She looked at him. 'I think there's been some kind of mistake.'

He blinked. 'You're not in charge of Tonielli's?'

'Oh, I'm in charge, all right.' She folded her arms. 'But the business isn't for sale.'

He looked shocked. As well he might—a shark in a business suit, who'd planned to buy her grandfather's ice-cream empire at a rock-bottom price.

A handsome shark—Carenza would give him that—with dark hair brushed back from his face, a generous mouth and beautiful dark eyes. A sexy shark, even. But he was still a shark. And she wasn't selling. Not to him, not to anyone.

'You're going to run Tonielli's?' he asked.

Carenza had seen that incredulous expression before. On her new boss's face, when she'd made a suggestion about running the gallery. Just before she'd walked out; no way could she work with someone who treated her like an airhead, incapable of doing anything other than giggling, answering the phone and painting her nails. And it needled her that this man—a man she'd never even met before—clearly also thought that she was an airhead. Why wouldn't he take her seriously?

Because she was blonde?

Or because she was a woman and Dante Romano was an Italian man, incredibly chauvinistic and still stuck in the attitudes of the nineteen fifties?

'I'm going to run it,' she said, keeping her voice ice-cool.

He leaned back in his chair. 'How?'

She lifted her chin and narrowed her eyes at him. 'Don't be insulting.'

'Signorina Tonielli, you have no experience and the business is in a mess,' he said quietly. 'It needs turning around—and I have the knowledge and the staff to do that.'

He was bluffing, she was sure. Things weren't that bad. She shrugged. 'There's a recession on. Everyone's feeling the bite.'

'The business is in trouble, and I think it's more than just the recession. And you don't have the experience or the staff to fix things.'

'Signor Romano, you know nothing about me.' She folded her arms. 'You're assuming that I'm not capable of running the business my family started five generations ago.'

'Not just running it. Taking it out of the red and moving it into this century.'

Red. Exactly what she was seeing, right now, after his smug, pompous remarks. 'You think I'm too stupid to do that?'

'Too inexperienced,' he corrected.

'And what makes you think I'm inexperienced?' she shot back.

And then she realised what she'd said. How it could be interpreted. Especially as his gaze travelled over her very, very slowly, from the top of her head down to desk level—and then all the way back again. Assessing her. Appraising her. And he clearly liked what he saw.

To her mortification, she felt the colour seep into her cheeks.

Anyone would think she was sixteen, not twenty-eight.

Sixteen, and experiencing her very first interested look from a man.

If Dante Romano had looked at her like that when she was sixteen, she would've been a complete puddle of hormones. As it was, her body was already reacting, and she was very glad she'd worn a business suit; the thick material of her jacket would hide the fact that her nipples were hardening.

This was so inappropriate, it was untrue. This was *business*. She shouldn't even be thinking about sex. A year ago, she would've done more than just think about it. But she was putting that mixed-up part of her life behind her now. She had the chance to start all over again.

Then he spoke, and it was as if he'd thrown a bucket of icy water over her. 'Have you ever done a real day's work in your life?'

What? For a moment, she was too surprised and angry to speak. He thought she was the kind of woman who did nothing but party and live off the allowance her grandfather gave her? OK, she'd admit that it had been true enough, ten years ago. But she'd grown up a lot since then. And, until Amy had retired through ill health and sold the gallery, Carenza had most definitely had a job in London. She'd worked damned hard at it.

Striving to keep her voice cool, not wanting him to know how near she was to throwing her glass of water in his face, she drawled, 'As a matter of fact, I have.'

'In an art gallery.'

He knew that? Well, of course. If you were planning to buy out a business, you'd want to know exactly what you were getting for your money. He'd obviously done his research on the business—and on her. Except he hadn't done it thoroughly enough, or he'd know that she was back for good and she wasn't planning to sell.

In the second before he masked his expression, Carenza could see exactly what he thought. That her job in the art gallery wasn't a real job—that it was a cushy number for a pampered girl from a wealthy family. That was what the new gallery owner had thought, too. And it wasn't true. She lifted her chin. 'All businesses are run the same way.'

'Are they, now.' It wasn't a question.

He clearly believed she wasn't up to running Tonielli's. Well, he'd find out the hard way that he was wrong. She was going to do this. More than that, she was going to do this *well*.

'I don't think we have anything more to say to each other, Signor Romano.' She stood up. 'Thank you for the drink of water. Good morning.' And she walked out of his office with her head held high.

CHAPTER TWO

IT WAS good to be home. Back in Naples after ten years away—one spent travelling the world, nine based in London. To live near the sea again, to see the harbour with the little fishing boats and yachts bobbing up and down on the water and the city stretching up the hill from the sea-front. The pole by the white rocks in front of the Castel dell'Ovo, where lovers attached a lock with their names scrawled on it in marker pen, making a huge impromptu sculpture that grew and changed every week. The band-stand in the Villa Comunale with its pretty wrought-iron skeleton, orb lights and striped glass awning. The sun set-ting behind the island of Ischia, turning the sea a heathery purple and the sky a soft rose. And the brooding, broken peak of Vesuvius overshadowing everything.

Now she was back, Carenza realised how much she'd missed it all. Missed the taste of the sea air, missed the sight of the narrow alleyways festooned with flags and wash-ing, missed the scent of proper pizza instead of the stuff that passed for it in London.

Home.

Except it wasn't quite like before, when she'd been a carefree teen. Now she was in charge of Tonielli's. The fifth generation—sixth, if you were being picky—with a whole load of responsibility.

She went through the figures for the fourth time that day, and she still couldn't get them to add up. Her head was starting to throb, so she leaned her elbows on her desk, rested her chin in her hands and rubbed her temples with the tips of her fingers, trying to ease the ache. She was beginning to think that maybe Dante Romano had been right. She didn't have the experience to deal with this.

But what option did she have?

Sure, she could go back to Nonno and tell him she couldn't handle it. But that would feel like throwing his generosity back in his face. Her grandfather had believed in her enough to let her take over from him and run the business. And he was seventy-three, now. It was time he enjoyed his retirement, pottering around in the garden and meeting his friends in *caffès* instead of having all the stress of the business on his shoulders. Just as he would've done years ago, had her parents not been killed in that car crash. She sighed. No, handing Tonielli's back wasn't an option.

She couldn't ask Amy for advice, either. Sure, her former boss would help—but Carenza knew that Amy had just gone through another course of chemotherapy. The last thing Amy needed right now was this kind of stress. So Carenza really couldn't lean on her, either.

There was Emilio Mancuso, who, according to her grandfather, had been acting as the manager of the business for a while, but Carenza didn't feel comfortable with him. She couldn't put her finger on why—he'd always been perfectly polite to her, if a bit condescending—but there was something about him that made her feel wary. She didn't want to ask him for help. All her instincts told her that would be a bad idea.

None of her friends her own age ran a business, so she couldn't ask them for advice.

Which left…

She sighed. Nobody.

You have no experience and the business is in a mess.

Dante Romano was right about that.

It needs turning around.

He was right about that, too.

And I have the knowledge and the staff to do that.

The obvious answer was to sell the family business to him. But, if she did that, she'd be letting Nonno down. Breaking the family tradition. The last generation of the Toniellis, selling out. How could she do that?

Unless...

She smiled wryly. No, that was crazy. He'd never agree to that.

How do you know unless you ask? a little voice said inside her head.

Maybe. But was he as good as he said he was? Could he help her fix the business?

She pushed the papers to one side and drew her laptop closer, so she could look him up online. Dante Romano. Interestingly, there were no paparazzi shots of him with beautiful women. Or men, for that matter—but her gaydar was pretty accurate. That zing of attraction she'd felt towards him yesterday had been mutual, judging by the way he'd looked at her across his desk.

No stories about an acrimonious divorce, either. Hmm. So it looked as if Dante Romano steered clear of relationships and focused on his work.

A workaholic, then.

She looked him up on the business pages. Make that a very successful workaholic, she corrected herself. He had a chain of six restaurants at the age of thirty—pretty impressive, given that he seemed to have come from absolutely nowhere. A little more digging gave her the information that he had a solid track record of buying up businesses and then turning them round. And there was a new rumour in the business world that he was going to franchise his restaurants. Carenza didn't know much about franchising, but she had a feeling that it meant going national or even international—so Dante Romano would be way too busy to date anyone, right now.

Not that she was interested in his love life. At all. Because she wasn't going to act on the attraction between them. Right now, she didn't want to get involved with anyone. She wanted to concentrate on the family business—on feeling that she could do something worthwhile. Get her self-respect back. But would this franchising thing mean that he'd be too busy to help her? And, even if he wasn't, would he agree to be her mentor—to help her get the business back under control?

It was a risky strategy, she knew, but she had no other real choice. And there was only one way to find out if he'd help her.

Given that he was a workaholic, it was a fair bet that Dante would still be at his office. Her hand was shaking as she punched the number into the phone. 'Come on, Caz. Don't be such a wimp,' she told herself as she pressed the last digit. But with each ring of the phone, her nerves increased. Maybe she'd made a mistake. Maybe he wasn't there. Maybe she should just give u—

'Dante.' His voice was crisp, clear—and every coherent thought went out of her head.

'Hello?'

Get a grip, Caz, she told herself and took a deep breath. 'Signor Romano? It's Carenza Tonielli.'

'How can I help you, Signorina Tonielli?'

If he was surprised—or if he'd expected her to call and say she'd changed her mind, once she'd had a proper look through the books—it didn't show. He was polite, formal and absolutely expressionless. Which unnerved her even more.

'I, um, wondered if we could talk. There's something I wanted to run by you.'

'Where and when?'

He certainly didn't waste any time. Maybe that was why he was so good at business. 'My office?' As for when… 'When would be convenient for you?'

'Now?'

'Now?' She almost squeaked the word into the phone. Whoever had a business meeting at this time of the evening?

Then again, she didn't need any more time to prepare. There wasn't anything she could add to make her case. 'OK. Um, do you know where my office is?'

'Yes.'

Stupid question. Of course he did. He'd been planning to buy the business. No doubt he'd met her grandfather here. 'Good. I'll, um, see you in a bit, then.'

'Ciao.'

Her hand was still shaking slightly when she put the phone down. Well, she'd done it now. She was going to have to go through with it. Anyway, what was the worst thing that could happen? Just that he'd refuse. And if he did that, she'd still be in the same position she was in now. It wouldn't make things any more difficult. So it was ridiculous to feel so nervous about seeing him.

She busied herself shaking coffee grounds into a cafetière and boiling the kettle. She'd just rearranged the cups on the tray for the third time when she heard the knock at the shop door.

'Thank you for coming, Signor Romano,' she said as she let him in and locked the door behind him.

'Prego.' Still perfectly polite and formal. And his face

was even less easy to read than his voice. Maybe she should've asked him over the phone, instead. It would be a lot easier without those piercing eyes watching her every movement.

'May I offer you some coffee?' she asked as she led him through to her office.

'Thank you. No milk or sugar.'

Easy enough. She could do this.

Except her hand shook as she brought his cup over to the desk, and she spilled coffee all over his suit trousers.

'Oh, I'm so sorry! I didn't mean to—'

He cut her off with a shrug. 'No problem. It'll come out in the wash.'

But he was unsmiling. Grim, even. And her heart sank. Why had she ever been daft enough to think he was going to agree to this? It wasn't just a risky strategy, it was an insane one.

'So what did you want to run past me?' he asked.

She placed her own coffee very carefully on her desk and sat down. 'I've looked at Nonno's books.'

'And?'

'And you have a point. I admit it. I don't have the experience to turn things round. But—' she sucked in a breath '—if you'd agree to mentor me, I could do it.'

'Mentor you.' Again, his voice and his face were completely expressionless. She had no idea whether he was amused, outraged, surprised, interested. Definitely not a man to play poker against.

And then he was silent.

Thinking about it, maybe. Did she interrupt, or give him space, or what?

'What's in it for me?' he asked eventually.

'How about, you can say "I told you so" and feel really, really smug?'

That earned her a smile, and maybe the slightest soften-ing in those beautiful dark eyes—which gave her enough heart to continue. 'Seriously, I can pay you to mentor me,' she said. 'Tell me what you charge.'

'More than you can afford, Princess. Remember, I've already seen your books.'

Princess? That rankled. But she could hardly have a hissy fit on him. Not if she wanted him to help her.

'I can pay you,' she insisted.

'How?'

She took a deep breath. 'I could...' She licked her lower lip. She could sell her jewellery. It would hurt—especially parting with the watch that her grandparents had given her for her twenty-first—but if she could save the business and make her grandparents proud of her, it would be worth it.

He clearly mistook her pause, because he raised an eye-brow. 'I'm thirty years old. I've never had to pay for sex before, Princess, and I have no intention of starting now.'

'I d-didn't mean *that*,' she stuttered, feeling her face flood with colour. 'I was going to say, I can sell some of my jewellery.'

Except now he'd put a picture in her head. One that was even more inappropriate than the one that had been there the last time she'd met him. A picture of him naked, in her bed. Buried deep inside her.

Oh, help. She really needed to get a grip. This was about *business*.

'Why?' he asked.

'Why?' *Think, Caz, think.* Except she didn't have a clue what he was talking about. The circuits in her brain had just scrambled.

'Why do you want me to mentor you?'

Oh. Yes. The reason she'd asked him here in the first place. The reason that should've been uppermost in her mind. Except that picture in her head had got in the way. Big time. She took a deep breath. 'I'm asking you to mentor me because you have experience at turning businesses round.' She listed the last three restaurants he'd bought, and the dates.

He raised an eyebrow. 'Done your homework, then, Princess?'

'Don't call me that!' She glared at him.

Then she remembered. She was asking him a favour. She had to play nice. 'Please,' she added belatedly. 'My name's Carenza.'

'Carenza.' It sounded like a caress, the way he said it. All deep and husky and sexy as hell.

No. She had to focus.

'You were right, Signor Romano. I don't have the experience to turn the business round.'

'And you're eating humble pie.' He inclined his head. 'Interesting.'

'Why do you have such a low opinion of me?' she asked.

'Because I know your type.' He paused, giving her a measured look. 'Princess.'

It took all her effort not to glower at him. 'I'm not a princess,' she said coolly.

'Put your feet on the desk.'

She frowned. 'What?'

'Put your feet on the desk,' he repeated.

She had no idea what he was driving at, but she did as he requested.

'Look at your shoes. High-end designer brand. They'd cost almost a month's wages for most of your staff,' he said softly. 'So are you going to tell me now that you're not a princess?'

Put like that, it sounded bad. She took her feet off the

desk. 'I had a job in England,' she said, knowing that she sounded defensive.

'Uh-huh.'

So he really did think it had been no more than a sinecure. 'I wasn't just sitting there filing my nails and fluttering my eyelashes. I was Amy's PA. I organised things. I know how retail works.'

'For luxury goods, maybe, but not food. It's a completely different customer base,' he pointed out.

'Look, I've admitted that I need help. What more do you expect from me?'

'Take the easy way out. Sell the business to me.'

She shook her head. 'I can't do that.'

'Why not?'

'Because I'm the fifth generation of Toniellis. It's up to me to make this work.' She swallowed hard. 'I guess I would've been the sixth generation. Or maybe if my parents had lived, I'd have had a brother or sister to share the burden of the business with me.' She shook herself. 'But you can't change the past, so it's pointless brooding over it. You just have to get on with things.'

Dante looked at her. She wouldn't sell because the business had been part of her family's life for years. So she had family loyalty after all. Given how few times she'd been back to Italy in the last ten years, he'd thought she'd pretty much abandoned her grandparents, happy with a life of partying in London. And she'd gone seriously off the rails last year.

But maybe Carenza Tonielli was turning over a new leaf. Maybe she wasn't quite what he'd thought she was.

And, if she really wanted to make the business work, then getting a mentor to teach her the ropes would be the best thing that she could do.

She'd chosen him. Ironic, as he'd planned to buy her out.

He could refuse—but, then again, he owed Gino. The old man had given him a break, all those years ago. Gino had given Dante solid advice, taught him things that had stood him in good stead in business. This was Dante's chance for payback: to help Gino's granddaughter and make sure that the *gelati* business didn't go under.

And this had nothing to do with the fact that Carenza had the most beautiful mouth and the bluest eyes he'd ever seen. Or the fact that he could imagine that glorious blonde hair spread over his pillow, her lips parted and her body arched in pleasure as he touched her.

'OK,' he said abruptly.

She blinked. 'What?'

He rolled his eyes. 'Pay attention, Princess.' He wasn't going to call her 'Signorina Tonielli', not if he was going to be her mentor. But he wasn't going to call her by her given name, either. It would be too intimate. This way, he could keep some distance between them. Maybe it would keep his wayward thoughts under control, too. He wasn't used to feeling anything less than in full control of himself, and it unnerved him slightly that Carenza Tonielli could have this effect on him. He pushed the unwanted attraction away. This was *business*. 'I said OK, I'll be your mentor.'

Her face was flooded with relief. 'Thank you. But I meant it about paying you. I can't expect you to do this for nothing. I mean, I'm taking your time.'

'No payment required. I'll give you guidance, where I can—but you're going to be the one doing the work, not me.'

'Thank you. I appreciate that.' She sat up straight. 'Where do we start?

'You can start,' he said, 'by wearing something frumpy.'

* * *

Carenza could see from the shock on Dante's face that he hadn't actually meant to say that. So she wasn't the only one with pictures in her head, then?

The room suddenly felt way, way too small—and it felt as if all the oxygen had just been sucked out of it, too, for good measure.

'What's wrong with my business suit?' she asked, her voice only just above a whisper.

'Nothing. The jacket and skirt are fine.' There was a slash of colour over his cheekbones.

So what was bothering him? Her top? Her shoes? Anger flared. The woman she'd been last year wouldn't have thought twice about taking off her jacket, strutting round to his side of the desk and teasing him, and she could see in his face that he thought he knew her type; his research must've dredged up a hell of a lot of dirt. No wonder he wasn't taking her seriously. *Well, let's play your little game, Signor Romano, then I'll show you just how wrong you are about me when I turn you down cold.*

She stood up, slid the jacket off her shoulders and rested it over the back of her chair. 'Is this the problem?' She fingered the spaghetti straps.

His eyes were very, very dark. 'You're playing with fire, Princess.'

'You started it,' she pointed out. 'So what's the problem with my top?'

He swallowed hard. 'You're asking me?'

'You're the one with the problem.'

He raked a hand through his hair. 'OK. If you really want to know…it's distracting.'

So was he. Especially because tonight there was the faintest hint of stubble on his face—and it made her want to touch. It made her want to know how it would feel against her skin. 'Distracting, how?'

'I thought I was supposed to be the one asking the questions?'

'Distracting, how?' she repeated.

'Because it's designed to make a man wonder if you're wearing anything underneath it.'

This time there was a definite challenge in his gaze. Hot. Sultry. She could see how much he wanted her. OK, so it was mutual. But she could keep her head. Push him that little bit further. She gave a half-shrug. 'There's only one way to find out.'

His breathing was fast, shallow. Just like hers.

'Show me,' he whispered.

The words were soft, sweet as honey and sexy as sin. The ultimate temptation. Yeah. She could play this game. And then she'd stop—because she could.

She pushed one spaghetti strap down her shoulder. Then the other. Adrenalin throbbed through her veins. Would he make a move now?

But he was waiting.

Not patiently. The tension was coming off him in waves. Any second now his control would snap. Any second...

'Show me,' he repeated.

This was where she was supposed to switch it back to him. Beckon. Let him come and find out for himself.

But her body wasn't paying any attention whatsoever to her head. She couldn't think of a smart retort. All she could think of was how much she wanted him. Wanted *this*. So she found herself pulling the stretchy top down. Little by little. Every millimetre of skin she uncovered felt unbearably sensitive. Tingling. Worse still, she wanted him to touch her. Desperately. She needed to feel his hands on her skin. His mouth.

The top was pushed down round her waist, now, proving to him that she was wearing a bra. One without straps. Lacy and black, to match her top.

'So now you know,' she said shakily.

'Yes.' He moistened his lower lip. 'We still have a problem.'

She knew that. Her breasts felt heavy. Aching. If he didn't touch her right now, she was going to implode. 'Dante,' she whispered. 'Please.'

A millisecond later, he was round her side of the desk and his mouth was jammed over hers. It felt less like a kiss than a declaration of war—and he wasn't going to take any prisoners. Which was fine by her. She didn't want him to. She needed this—and she needed it now.

His fingers dealt with the hook on her bra in a nanosecond, and she couldn't help a moan of pleasure when he let it drop to the floor and cupped her breasts. Strong yet sensitive hands. Gorgeous hands. And she wanted more. His thumbs circled her nipples, teasing her and driving her just that little bit more crazy. Her breasts felt so tight; she really wanted his mouth there to ease the ache. She pushed against him, telling him with her body exactly what she needed.

He dragged his mouth from hers, then slowly kissed his way down her throat.

She really was going to go insane if he kept this up. If he made her wait a single second more. She pushed her fingers through his hair—so soft and silky against her skin—and dragged his head down to where she wanted it. She shuddered as his mouth closed over one nipple and sucked. 'Dante. *Yes.*' The word dragged out in a hiss of desire.

Then she felt his hand moving her skirt upwards. She changed her stance slightly to make it easier for him—and so he'd get there quicker, too, because she really needed this.

She sighed in pleasure as he stroked her inner thigh, and then his hand cupped her sex. Only the thin barrier of her knickers was between them now and that felt way, way too much. She needed to be skin to skin with him. Right here, right now.

As if he could read her mind, he hooked the material to one side. His finger stroked along the length of her sex, and she rocked against him. And then, oh, bliss, he pushed a finger inside her. She nearly cried with relief, it felt so good.

He was kissing her again, and she was kissing him back, pushing her tongue against his and rocking against his hand.

His thumb found her clitoris; as he touched her, it felt as if she were going up in flames.

And then, shockingly, she was coming. Harder and faster than she could ever remember.

The climax left her drained; all the tension and misery of the last few days were simply washed away in a rush of desire.

And then she became aware of just where they were. Standing next to her desk. Her top was pushed down round her waist, her skirt was hiked up to meet it, his hand was in her knickers…Whereas he was fully clothed. Not a thing out of place. Completely in control—while hers was in tiny, tiny shreds.

She closed her eyes. 'Oh, God.'

He gently caught her lower lip between his teeth. 'What's the matter, Princess?' he whispered against her mouth.

She felt like a tart. 'You know,' she whispered back.

'Mind-reading isn't one of my skills, I'm afraid.' There was an amused glitter in his eyes. 'You'll have to be a little more specific.'

He really wasn't going to let her get away with this,

was he? She'd just have to try to brazen it out. 'It's just a bit awkward. You're fully dressed—and I'm...' Practically naked.

'You look pretty good to me, right now.' He stole a kiss. 'But you have a point. This isn't what mentoring is supposed to be about.' He removed his hand from her knickers, restored order to her skirt and slid the straps of her top back up her arms.

She grabbed her jacket and shoved it on—even though she knew that it was pretty much closing the stable door after the horse had bolted.

He knew it, too. Because he was smiling.

She glared at him. 'Don't you laugh at me.'

'I'm not.' His smile broadened. 'OK. I admit, I'm laughing at you just a little bit. Putting on that jacket isn't going to stop me remembering what you look like without it, Princess.'

It wasn't doing anything to stop her remembering what it felt like to be practically naked in his arms, either. Or how he'd just stroked her to a quicker climax than she'd ever achieved in her entire life.

'I'll wear something frumpy, next time,' she muttered. 'And then we'll both be able to concentrate.'

'Sure.' Though his expression was saying something else entirely. *Don't bet on it.*

What the hell had she just started?

'My office. Eight o'clock tomorrow night,' he said. 'Your email address?'

She had just enough brain cells working to let her scribble it down on a piece of paper.

'Good. I'll email you some things to work on before then.'

And then he was gone. Making her feel more like a tart than ever. He'd thought she was propositioning him, when she hadn't been. And then…she'd thrown herself at him. Practically stripped for him. So much for thinking she could prove him wrong about her. She'd just reinforced every single prejudice he had about her.

Talk about a mistake. She hadn't learned a thing. Dante Romano wasn't even her type. She normally went for refined, arty, intellectual types. Not brooding men whose thought processes were so far away from her own that she didn't have a clue what was going on in their heads.

OK, so he was drop-dead gorgeous. But that still didn't mean she should've thrown herself at him like that. And the fact that she hadn't dated anyone over the past year was no excuse at all.

She covered her face in her hands. Tomorrow, she'd have a cold shower before she went to his office. A very *long* cold shower. And maybe she'd be able to keep this damned attraction under control long enough to get him to take her seriously and save her grandfather's business.

CHAPTER THREE

DANTE scowled at his computer.

His concentration was shot to pieces, and it was all Carenza Tonielli's fault.

Well, maybe not *all* hers. He could've said no.

And he definitely shouldn't have said that about her clothes being distracting. Because knowing exactly what she looked like under them—and what her skin felt like against his mouth—was a damn sight more distracting than what he'd imagined.

For pity's sake. He didn't have *time* for this. And he didn't want to get involved with a high-maintenance woman who'd demand his time and his complete attention, and have hissy fits all over the place when she didn't get her own way.

What had just happened between them definitely wasn't going to be repeated.

And he wasn't going to let himself wonder about how it would be to sink into her warm, sweet depths. To feel her body tightening round his. To...

'Oh, just get on with it and *focus*,' he told himself sharply, and opened up his email.

He dealt with the first three messages as economically as he could. But he couldn't stop thinking about Carenza.

And it really annoyed him that he'd lost control like that, instead of keeping things businesslike.

OK. Obviously he needed to get this over with so he could get her out of his head. He opened a new email.

Tomorrow, bring your USP and competitor analysis.

That was better. To the point, businesslike—and mentorlike.

Right. Now he could go back to his business. Focused, the way he always was.

And then his computer beeped.

The email was from Carenza.

USP???

He rolled his eyes and hit the reply button.

Unique selling proposition. What makes you different from the competition.

He thought about it after he'd sent it. Clearly she wouldn't have a clue about competitor analysis, either. He added another email.

Change of plan. I'll pick you up at 4 p.m. tomorrow and do the first competitor analysis with you as a blueprint.

A very humble reply arrived:

Thank you very much.

Strictly speaking, he already had enough on his plate.

Franchising Dante's was going to take all his time, and then some. Carenza Tonielli and sorting out the *gelati* business were distractions he really didn't need.

But he felt he owed Gino, for giving him that first break.

He pushed away the thought that it wasn't the only reason he'd agreed to mentor her, and sent her another email.

Dress like a tourist. See you at 4.

Dress like a tourist. Which meant…what? Carenza wondered, the following morning. Last night, he'd said he wanted her to dress like a frump.

Just before his hand had been in her knickers.

At her instigation. Even though she'd intended to stop well before then.

This was bad. Really bad. She needed to clear things up before she could face him again. And she couldn't possibly ring him. It was too, too embarrassing to speak about. She took refuge in the distance of an email.

About last night…I don't normally do that sort of thing. Can we please pretend it didn't happen?

He made her wait for an hour before he replied.

Which bit?

Oh, now that was unfair. He knew very well what she meant. Clearly he was going to extract every gram of humiliation out of this.

Not the mentoring. The other bit.

And she wasn't going to write *that* down.

O. Sure.

Her face flamed. She knew he'd deliberately missed off the h. A big O, indeed. He was obviously enjoying this. She'd just bet there'd been a big, fat, mocking grin on his face as he'd typed that, and it made her want to punch him.

At the same time, she was aware that last night had been really one-sided. That she'd been the only one who'd climaxed. She'd simply taken everything he was prepared to give.

And she didn't normally act like that. She hadn't even dated since last year—since those terrible few months where she'd gone completely off the rails and slept with way too many Mr Wrongs. Her friends all said she'd gone too far the other way now and was too picky, but the men who'd asked her out had bored her. They'd been too fond of their own reflections in the mirror. And she was tired of getting involved with men who didn't meet her needs. It was easier just to have fun with her friends and forget about relationships. Besides, she had a feeling that Tonielli's was going to take up all her energies for the foreseeable future.

And Dante Romano was her mentor. *Just* her mentor. This was business. They'd agreed to forget about last night.

So just what did tourists wear? Frumpy ones, in particular? She didn't actually own anything frumpy—and, given the state of the books, it wasn't a good idea to go anywhere near a clothes shop to buy something especially for this afternoon. Not even a charity shop. In the end, she compromised with jeans and a little cardigan over one of her favourite strappy tops, and pulled her hair back into a neat ponytail. She thought about the shoes, then slid on a pair of her favourite designer heels. Being a tourist didn't mean that you had to wear flip-flops or scuzzy trainers, did it?

Dante called for her at four on the dot, and she had to fight to keep her jaw closed. When he was a shark in a suit, she could just about cope with him. But what he was wearing made her want to rip his clothes off him right there and then. A black vest T-shirt, a pair of faded denims that looked incredibly soft and touchable, a black leather jacket and a pair of suede desert boots—topped off with a pair of dark glasses. He hadn't shaved since yesterday. His hair was slightly rumpled—enough to tell her that it curled when it was wet.

And the bad boy look really, *really* suited him.

'Ready?' he asked.

'Uh.' She couldn't actually get a word out. Getting air back in her lungs was a bit of a problem, too.

'Uh?' He gave her a mocking smile. 'Does that mean yes or no, Princess?'

'It means we have a problem,' she mumbled.

'What?'

'The way you're dressed.'

He raised an eyebrow. 'Too scruffy for you, Princess?'

No. Too damn sexy. And she didn't dare answer him—just in case she ended up admitting that she wanted to lock her office door, tear his clothes off, and do him. On her desk. That very second.

How had she ever thought that she could cope with Dante Romano being just her mentor?

Instead, she chickened out. 'Why do we have to dress like tourists?'

'Because people in business suits don't go for ice cream at four p.m. They're too busy working.'

'Oh.'

He took pity on her. 'We can hardly visit one of your

competitors and make notes while we're sitting there, Princess.'

'Why not? They won't know the notes are about them.'

'Trust me, it's easier this way. It's called "mystery shopping". They do it all the time in the retail trade—to check out the competition as well as making sure that their own staff are doing the right thing. We go as ordinary customers, we get treated like ordinary customers—and then you'll know what their service standards are like.'

'Isn't that spying?'

'No. You're looking at what they offer, what they do better than you, and what they do worse than you, so you can tweak your own business and offer your customers more.'

'Uh-huh.' And that was another problem.

It must've shown on her face, because he sighed. 'You haven't analysed your own business, have you?'

'Not yet. I've only been back in Italy for a few weeks. But I can do it.' She folded her arms. 'I'm not an airhead.'

'No, Princess.'

She heard the sarcasm in his tone, and glowered at him. 'You're judging me when you hardly know me.'

'Look, we don't have time to arg—oh, forget it. We'll do this the quick way.' He yanked her into his arms and kissed her. Hard. Hot. Demanding. To the point where she ended up kissing him back and pressing herself against him, with her arms wrapped round his neck.

When he broke the kiss, her pulse rate had practically doubled and her thoughts were completely scrambled. Hadn't they agreed earlier that they were going to forget last night? He'd just—just… She dragged in a breath. Her body was definitely happy about this, but her head wasn't. 'What the hell was that for?' she demanded.

'Right now, we're tourists. You're my girlfriend.' He shrugged. 'I thought I'd help you get into the part.'

Get into the part? How the hell did he expect her to concentrate after he'd just kissed her like that and turned her
brain to mush?

It got worse when they were halfway down the street,
because he took her hand. Exactly as if she really were his
girlfriend and they were just out for a stroll, exploring the
sights of Naples.

Her skin tingled where he touched her. Was it the same
for him? Or was he mentally totting up balance sheets and
working on business plans? Not that she was going to ask—
even if she'd been able to get the words out—because she
didn't want him knowing just how much he distracted her.
Especially as she had a nasty feeling that she didn't distract
him at all.

'Pay attention, Princess,' he said, as if he'd guessed anyway, and held the door of an ice cream parlour open for her.

And then things got even worse. She knew she was supposed to be making mental notes about the *gelateria*. What
was good about it, what wasn't so good, where it was different from her own shops. But for the life of her she couldn't
concentrate when he insisted on feeding her a spoonful
of the ice cream sundae he'd ordered—because she could
imagine him feeding her ice cream like this somewhere
else.

Naked.

In her bed.

'You're supposed to return the favour, Princess,' he murmured, and her skin heated.

Did he mean favour as in what he'd done for her last
night? Or as in the ice cream?

Taking the cowardly option, she fed him a spoonful of
ice cream.

'Gorgeous,' he purred, giving her the sexiest smile she'd

ever seen. Hinting that she was gorgeous, not just the ice cream.

If he kept this up, she was going to need oxygen therapy.

And she was pretty sure he was doing this on purpose. To tease her. Or maybe to prove that she was an airhead who couldn't concentrate—just as she'd been last night.

She gritted her teeth, and forced herself to focus on the shop. On the menu. The décor. The service.

The waitress brought the bill over to them; her smile was all for Dante, and Carenza was truly shocked to feel a flicker of jealousy.

For pity's sake. She had no call on Dante Romano at all. He was her business mentor. For all she knew, he could be involved with someone.

Though she didn't think he was. Otherwise last night wouldn't have happened. One thing she'd already worked out about Dante Romano was that he had a strict code of honour. He'd never cheat.

'My bill.' She scooped it up.

He shook his head. 'You might do this kind of thing in England, but this is Italy. I'm paying.'

'And I'm half English,' she reminded him. 'This is the twenty-first century. I'm paying.'

She won by the simple expedient of taking the bill and going up to the counter before he could grab the bill back from her.

'You're difficult,' he said, when she returned.

And he wasn't? She shrugged. 'You're the one who calls me "Princess".'

'Let's go for a stroll.' He held the door open for her, and they walked in silence to railings overlooking the sea.

He leaned against the railings, his legs slightly apart. 'Come here.'

'Why?'

He rolled his eyes. 'Because you're still supposed to be in role.'

She took a step nearer.

He coughed. 'And my girlfriend's really going to stand as far away from me as she possibly can. Not.'

She took another step closer, and he reached out to pull her nearer still, so she was standing between his legs and his hand was resting lightly on her hip.

'So what did you think of the shop?'

Standing this close to him, she was finding it hard to concentrate. How the hell could he talk about business and keep it all straight in his head while he was holding her like this?

'It's called multi-tasking, Princess. A very useful business asset.'

She groaned. 'Did I just say that out loud?'

'Yup.'

'I lied.'

He glanced down at her top. 'Try telling your nipples that. They're standing to attention.'

'I think I hate you.'

He laughed. 'Then concentrate. Tell me what you thought about the shop.'

'The ice cream was good. The service was fine. The prices are about the same as mine. Oh, and the décor was terrible.'

'What do they do that you don't?'

'I…have no idea,' she admitted. 'More flavours?'

'They offer sandwiches. Hot drinks. So they can keep tourists happy in the winter months.'

And then he staggered her by rattling off a detailed analysis of the shop. What it was doing wrong, what it was doing right, where it was beating her, where Tonielli's scored higher.

How had he got all that from just one little visit—a visit where he'd seemed to be paying more attention to her than anything else, flirting with her and feeding her ice cream from his spoon and getting her to do the same to him?

A skateboarder pushed past them, causing her to move closer to Dante. And then she discovered that her mentor wasn't quite as unaffected by her proximity as he claimed. He was definitely hard for her.

Wanting to get her own back—just a little bit—and knowing that she was seriously crossing a line here, she licked her lower lip. Slowly. She let her gaze drop to his mouth, then back up to his eyes. Well, to his sunglasses. But she was pretty sure he wasn't missing a trick behind those dark lenses.

'You're playing with fire, Princess,' he warned her.

She knew that. Her body remembered just how hot he was. 'About last night...'

'We agreed to forget it.'

'But I wasn't fair to you.' She'd taken her pleasure from him, and given him nothing in return. And that felt wrong.

'Uh-huh.'

'Lost for words, Dante?'

He gave her a slow, wicked smile. Leaned forward. Touched his mouth to hers.

And it was like lighting touchpaper.

She became dimly aware of catcalls and whistles from a group of passing teenagers, and pulled back from him. His mouth was swollen and reddened, and she'd just bet that hers was in the same state.

And she couldn't say a single thing.

'Now who's lost for words?' he asked.

She blew out a breath. 'This is supposed to be business. But.' She swallowed hard. 'You and me—this is getting in the way.'

'You said you were going to wear something frumpy. So we could both concentrate.'

She spread her hands. 'This is as frumpy as I get.'

He raised an eyebrow. 'Do-me heels and tight jeans?'

He was blaming *her* for this? 'You're the one wearing the do-me jacket and touchable denim.'

'Maybe you need to find yourself another mentor.'

'There isn't anyone else I can ask. If Nonno thinks I'm struggling, he'll take over again and that's not fair. He's seventy-three. He deserves a chance to relax with Nonna and have some fun.'

'What about your old boss in London?'

She shook her head. 'She's ill. It wouldn't be fair to ask her. And I'm not asking Emilio Mancuso.'

'What's wrong with him?'

'I...' She grimaced. 'Nothing I can put my finger on.'

'But your instincts tell you no.'

She nodded. 'So there's only you I can ask.'

'Scraping the bottom of the barrel, hmm?'

'No. You were my first choice. You know what you're doing. I could learn a lot from you.'

'But?'

She sighed. 'But it doesn't help when you turn up looking like sex on legs. When you feed me ice cream from your spoon and give me smouldering looks.'

He raised an eyebrow. 'Are you saying you want to do me, Princess?'

God, *yes*. She shivered. 'I don't normally behave like this.'

'No?'

So he *did* know about London. She felt her face redden. 'You provoked me.'

'Not *that* much. You could've called a halt at any time.'

Yes. Which was exactly what she'd planned to do. But

the touch of his skin against hers had pushed everything out of her head. Besides, it hadn't been completely one-sided. He'd started it. And if he was that uninterested, why was he touching her now? 'Your hands are still on my bottom,' she informed him. 'And there are...' She gave a delicate cough. 'Other signs, shall we say.'

'So there are.' He sighed. 'OK. I admit it. I have the hots for you. And, judging by last night, it's mutual.'

'We don't even like each other. You think I'm a spoiled princess.'

'You are. And, since we're telling it like it is, you think I'm...?'

'A workaholic. Someone who wouldn't know how to begin to have fun.'

'A dull boy, hmm?' He shrugged. 'Bottom line, Princess, this isn't going to work. You're looking for someone to give you a good time. And I don't have space in my life for someone who's going to stamp her foot every time I'm late for dinner, or when I don't want to go to a party because I have more important things to do with my time than listen to tedious people spouting their opinion about something they know nothing about, or talking drivel about trivial things.'

'I don't stamp my feet,' she said, glowering at him.

'Metaphorically, you're doing it right now.'

'So why did you agree to be my mentor?' She still didn't quite understand that.

'Because I owe Gino.'

'You owe Nonno? Why?'

'He gave me a break when I was younger, taught me a few things about business. So helping you out of trouble is kind of payback.'

She felt deflated. So he wasn't doing this because he liked her.

'You're right. I don't like you,' he agreed—as if she'd said it out loud. Or maybe it was written all over her face. 'I don't like what you stand for. The way you were quite happy to take your allowance and swan off round the world, then almost never came back to see your grandparents.'

'And how would you know anything about that?'

'Because I saw the wistfulness in Gino's face whenever he talked about you.'

Her grandfather had talked to Dante about her?

'He missed you.'

Guilt flooded through her. She hadn't been fair, but her grandparents had never complained. She didn't have to give him any explanation for her behaviour; but on the other hand she didn't want him to think she was completely self-ish and spoiled. 'I was eighteen, Dante. I knew there was a big wide world out there. I wanted to see it. I wanted to know what else there was outside Naples. So, yes, I trav-elled. I went to Rome, to Milan, to Paris. To Sydney and New York and LA.'

'Style capitals.' He didn't look impressed.

'Yes, I'll give you that. The fashion drew me, at first. But then I went to London. To meet my mother's family. To find out about that side of me. Wouldn't you have been curious, in my shoes? Wouldn't you have wanted to meet the side of the family you'd never met?'

That rather depended on what the family was like, Dante thought. He didn't want anything to do with his father's family. He'd seen more than enough destruction in the first fourteen years of his life and he didn't need to see any more. 'Maybe,' he said cagily.

'And I didn't desert my grandparents. I rang home three times a week. I sent pictures and emails.'

'Which isn't the same as being here.' He paused. 'What made you come back?'

'Primarily, Nonno and Nonna's golden wedding anniversary.' She sighed. 'And then I realised they were getting old. My English grandparents had other children and grandchildren to look after them, but Nonno and Nonna only had me. So I thought it was time to come home.'

'And take over the family business.'

She nodded. 'Because I'm the last of the Toniellis. I have to step up to the plate.'

It wasn't what she wanted to do. He could see that. Yet she wasn't ignoring her duty—and he approved of that.

'What about your job in the art gallery?'

'Amy retired—she was ill, and the gallery was too much of a burden. She sold it.'

'Didn't the new owner want to keep you on?'

She blew out a breath. 'Let's just say we didn't see eye to eye. So I guess it worked out for the best—I could leave and come back to Naples without letting anyone down.'

'What was the problem?'

'He treated me like an airhead. Which,' she said, 'I'm not. I could've done a degree.'

He gave a mirthless laugh. 'Pushing paper around and partying for three years?'

'No, a university education teaches you how to think.' She frowned. 'I take it you didn't go to university.'

'No. And I didn't miss a thing. I learned a lot more from life.'

'Didn't your parents want you to go?'

He didn't want to talk about his parents. 'No,' he said shortly. 'There's more to life than studying.'

'A minute ago, you were kissing me. Now, we're sniping at each other.' She shook her head, as if she didn't have a clue how it had started. 'Why are we fighting?'

'Because you don't understand where I'm coming from, and I don't understand you. It's like comparing…oh, apples and oranges. We're too different.' Though it didn't stop him wanting her. And he hated the fact that she could make his control slip.

'So what are we going to do about this?' she asked.

'About what?'

'You and me.'

'There is no you and me.'

She moved forward again, just far enough to brush against his erection. 'No?'

'There is no you and me,' he repeated through gritted teeth. He'd agree to mentor her. But it was hard to concentrate on this mentoring stuff when they couldn't even be in the same room without wanting to rip each other's clothes off.

'You're telling me,' she said dryly.

He groaned. 'Tell me I didn't say that out loud.'

'You did.' And she looked mightily pleased about it.

What was wrong with him? He never lost control like this. He'd spent years training himself to have absolute control over his feelings. To make sure that he didn't turn into his father.

But there was something about Carenza Tonielli. Something that made all his rules just beg to be broken. He bent his head to hers and kissed her again, enjoying the way she responded so hotly to him. The way she opened her mouth beneath his, letting him deepen the kiss. The way her hands curved over his buttocks, pulling him closer.

When he broke the kiss, her eyes were fever-bright and her mouth looked utterly lush. 'Why don't you just take me home, Princess?' he asked softly. 'Come home with me and do me.'

Her mouth parted. Delectably. Tempting. Perfect, even

white teeth; soft, perfect rosebud lips; and she made him ache. God, he wanted her. He couldn't remember wanting anyone this much in his entire life.

'Yes,' she whispered.

CHAPTER FOUR

THEY walked back towards his place in silence. Dante's head was telling him that this was a seriously bad plan, but his body was insistent that it was the best idea he'd had in years.

He realised that he was walking a bit too fast, given how high Carenza's heels were, and slowed his pace a bit to accommodate her. She gave him a grateful look.

'Sorry,' he muttered. And he had to look away from her before he did something really stupid. Like pinning her against the nearest wall and kissing her until they were both dizzy. The way he was feeling right now, they'd end up getting arrested for public indecency.

What was it about Carenza Tonielli that made him lose control like this?

And that made her the worst possible person he could be with. Because losing control absolutely wasn't an option for him. Not with his background. He couldn't afford to take that risk.

He still hadn't got himself completely back in control when she stopped him outside a pharmacy.

'What?' he asked.

'Supplies,' she said. 'Unless you already have some.'

Supplies? Then he realised what she meant. How the hell had that slipped his mind? 'Uh. No. I haven't. Wait here.'

He emerged with a pack of condoms in his pocket. It made him feel a bit like a schoolboy. Then he shook himself. This was simply getting rid of a distraction that was annoying both of them. Sex. Nothing more, nothing less. Once they'd got that out of the way, everything was going to be just fine. His head would be clear. So would hers. He'd help her fix her business and she'd be out of his life. No more complications.

The nearer they got to the restaurant, the more tense his muscles became.

Well, this had been his suggestion. Good or bad, he had to live with the consequences.

He went round to the side entrance and unlocked the door to let her in. It slammed behind them—and then everything bubbled over and his control snapped. He pinned her against the wall, kissing her hard. God, she was so soft, smelled so sweet...

And she was matching him kiss for kiss, bite for bite, hunger for hunger.

Dante wasn't sure how or when he'd done it, but he'd lifted Carenza and her legs were wrapped round his waist. He rocked his pelvis against hers and she moaned against his mouth. He could feel the heat of her sex through her jeans, and he just couldn't wait any more. He walked up the stairs with her still wrapped round him, not letting her go until he'd reached his bedroom; then slowly he let her slide to the floor, keeping her close to him so she'd be able to feel just how ready he was for her.

The next few moments were a blur. He had no idea who ripped whose clothes off, but at last they were naked. Skin to skin. As he'd wanted to be ever since she'd opened her mouth in the *gelateria* and let him feed her a spoonful of ice cream.

'Loosen your hair,' he said hoarsely.

She put one hand behind her head, took out the band holding her hair back, and shook her head so her hair fell over her shoulders.

'*Dio*, you're beautiful,' he said, the words torn from him. She transfixed him. He cupped her face and kissed her very, very softly before letting his hands mould to her shape, stroking down over her shoulders, pausing to cup her breasts and feel their weight in his hands, then slowly discovering the curve of her waist, the swell of her hips.

'Dante, I...' She licked her lower lip.

'What, Princess?' he asked softly.

Her breathing was fast and shallow, much like his own—and he could see it was an effort for her to speak. 'Do it now,' she begged. 'Before I go crazy.'

'Me, too,' he whispered. He had just enough sense left to grab the box of condoms from his pocket and rip open one of the foil packets.

'My job,' she said, taking it from him and sliding the condom over his erection.

He nearly yelped when she touched him, it felt so good.

She clearly guessed, because her smile was pure satisfaction. Smug, that she could have that effect on him.

Ha. Considering she'd been the one to come apart under his touch last night...

He kissed her hard, burying his hands in her hair. She kissed him back and rocked her pelvis against him. Impatient? Yeah, he knew how that felt. He needed to be inside her. He needed that more than he'd ever needed anything in his entire life.

At last she was lying beneath him on his bed, her hair spread out on his pillow, and he was inside her. Hot and wet and...pure heaven. He stayed still for a moment, letting her body adjust to him, and then began to move. Taking it slow and easy. Letting it build.

Her fingernails were running down his back, just hard enough for pleasure.

He shifted so that he could push deeper inside her.

'Oh, God, Dante, *yes*,' she murmured. 'More. More.' She pushed against him, increasing the pace and the pressure.

He felt her body start to ripple round him, and it tipped him into his own release. When he came, it was like seeing stars. Everything seemed to sparkle in his head. When he opened his eyes, he could see his feelings reflected in her eyes, that same sense of wonder. The whole world felt as if it had shifted.

He rolled off her and lay there beside her, utterly stunned. He'd thought they'd be good together, but not this good. Especially the first time.

Unless you counted last night as the first time.

But through the whole thing he'd felt completely in tune with her—and that worried him. He walked to the beat of his own drum. Nobody else's.

And then her hand found his; her fingers laced through his.

No, no, *no*. This was meant to be just sex. Not a relationship.

'I'd better deal with the condom,' he muttered, pulling his hand away from hers before he did something stupid. Like holding her hand right back.

When he came back from the bathroom, Carenza hadn't moved, other than to pull the sheet over her up to her waist. She really was gorgeous; he could feel his body stirring again at the sight of her.

And he didn't have a clue what to say. What she expected from him.

But then she smiled, shifted onto her side and patted the bed next to her.

Oh, hell. Now he knew exactly what she wanted. A cuddle. And to talk.

Well, he didn't want to talk. He didn't want to spill his guts to her. That wasn't who he was.

'Dante.' Her voice was very soft. 'You don't think I've finished with you yet, do you?' And in that split second she changed from princess to vamp.

Irresistible.

He climbed back onto the bed. 'OK, Princess, I'm in your hands.'

A flicker of hurt passed over her face. 'My friends call me Caz.'

'We're not exactly friends,' he pointed out.

'Let me rephrase that. People who are close to me.' She gave him a wry smile. 'And I don't think you can get much closer than you've just been.'

'No.' But physical closeness was where he drew the line. He didn't want emotional closeness. Didn't need it. He was fine just how he was, working hard and growing his business. Making his world secure. Emotional closeness was the quickest way to let the cracks grow and break that security. And no way was he ever going to let that happen.

'Am I that scary?' she asked.

'How do you mean, scary?'

'For a moment, there, you looked utterly terrified.'

Oh, hell. He always managed to mask his feelings. The fact that she could see right through him was worrying. In the extreme. 'It must've been your imagination,' he said coolly. 'I'm scared of nothing.' Not any more. His days of being scared were long behind him, left in the miseries of his childhood. 'I was thinking, as you're here I might as well feed you.'

'You're going to cook for me?'

He raised an eyebrow. 'When I have excellent chefs working for me downstairs? What's the point?'

'Oh.' She looked slightly crestfallen; then she glanced over at the crumpled trail of clothes across his bedroom.

He took pity on her. 'Don't worry, I'm not going to drag you down there.'

'Actually, I'd like to see your restaurant.'

'Not sitting with me, you won't—I don't want my staff talking about me.' The words were out before he could stop them.

To his relief, she didn't pick up on it. Because he sure as hell wasn't going to explain to her why he hated people talking about him.

'So what are you intending?' she asked.

'Room service. Kind of.'

She frowned. 'Surely that'll make them talk more?'

'I'm having a business discussion with a colleague and it ran a bit late, so we decided to take a break for dinner. It happens.'

'So what's the difference between them knowing I'm up here and seeing me downstairs with you?'

All the difference in the world. 'There just is, OK?'

'Dante, you're being completely illogical.'

He ignored her. 'Is there anything you're allergic to or hate eating, or shall we just have the special?'

'Special?'

'Dante's menu is the same, regardless of where the restaurant is, but then the chef at each restaurant has a corner of the menu that's just his or hers, a dish that's a local speciality or what have you,' he explained. 'It changes whenever the chef feels like it. That way my chef gets to enjoy the creative side and feels that he or she has an input to the menu.'

'Your staff really matter to you, don't they?' she asked.

'This is a service industry. Without your staff, you're nothing. You can produce the best food in the world, but if the service is poor the customer won't come back. So it's important that your staff feel they have a stake.'

She said nothing.

'You know nothing about your staff, do you?' he asked softly.

'Not yet,' she admitted.

'You need to know who works for you and what their job involves. The best way to do that is to spend a few hours doing every single job in your business, so you know the challenges your staff face and can empathise with them.'

'Is that what you did?'

He nodded. 'I still do it, every so often. It keeps me in touch with the staff and the business, and they respect me for it.'

'Every job?' she tested.

'Every job,' he emphasised, 'from waiting tables to pot-washing to cashing up last thing at night to peeling vegetables. And, yes, I clean toilets as well.'

'Right.' She looked utterly shocked.

Ha. He'd just bet she'd never cleaned a toilet in her life. And even when she'd been living in London, he was pretty sure that she hadn't cleaned her own flat. She would've paid someone to do it. Princesses didn't soil their hands.

'The special will be fine, thank you.' She paused. 'Um, would it be OK for me to have a shower?'

'Sure.' Dante had to hold back the idea of joining her in there. 'The bathroom's next door. There are clean towels in the airing cupboard. Help yourself to what you need.'

'Thank you.'

He scooped up his own crumpled clothes and headed for the kitchen to give her some privacy. While she was in the shower, he rang the restaurant and ordered the special.

He'd just switched the kettle on to make coffee when she walked in. She hadn't pulled her hair back again and his heart skipped a beat; like this, she looked younger than her twenty-eight years, slightly vulnerable.

And the thought hardened his heart. She didn't need his protection. She already had people looking out for her. Always had. Not like the way he'd been, half a lifetime ago.

'I've ordered the special. It should be with us in twenty minutes.'

'That'd be good. So does your chef recommend red or white?'

He shrugged. 'No idea. I don't drink.'

She blinked. 'What, not ever? Not even on your birthday or at Christmas?'

He thought back to his childhood. Christmases, his father's birthday. *Grappa*, followed by the anger and the pain and the tears. 'Not ever.' He forced himself to relax. It wasn't her fault that his father had been a mean drunk. 'But if you want wine, sure, I can order some.'

'No, water's fine by me.' She placed her hand on his arm. 'Dante, are you OK?'

'I'm fine,' he lied. 'Coffee?' He gave her his best professional smile.

'I…' For a moment, he thought she was going to argue. To push him. But then she gave in. 'Thanks. That'd be good.'

He busied himself making coffee. 'They'll buzz me when the food's ready. Come and sit down.'

Dante had just gone distant on her. And Carenza didn't have a clue why. She thought it might be something to do with his comment about not drinking. Ever. Was he a reformed alcoholic? If so, it must be difficult owning a restaurant chain; he probably had to eat out as part of his job, and every business meal she'd ever attended had always involved wine.

Though, since his barriers were well and truly up, she didn't feel that she could ask him.

This wasn't a relationship, she reminded herself. They were too different for it to work. She simply took the mug of coffee he offered her and followed him into his living room.

It was incredibly minimalist. There was a small dining table with four chairs; the laptop sitting on the table told her that he used the room as another office. There was a comfortable-looking sofa—but no television or games console, she noticed. And the picture on the wall looked as if a designer had chosen it for him. Bland, bland, bland.

There were no ornaments on the mantelpiece. Just a clock—and two photographs.

Knowing she was intruding, but unable to stop herself, she went over to take a closer look. One was of Dante with an older woman who looked enough like him to be his mother, and the other was a woman who might've been a couple of years older or younger than him, holding a baby. His sister, maybe? A cousin? Or maybe his mother holding him as a baby?

'Your family?' she asked.

'Yes.'

He didn't elaborate. And there was no sign of his father. Dead, like hers? Possibly not, or Dante would've had photographs, the precious last memories, as she did herself. Estranged? Never known him? Again, she couldn't ask. Dante was sending out 'off limits' signals all over the place.

Dante could see his flat through Carenza's eyes, and he didn't like what he saw. Boring. Stuffy. Minimalist.

But he didn't do ornaments. He'd seen his father smash too many of them in temper to want that kind of thing in his flat.

He wished she'd put the photographs down. He had a nasty feeling that she was going to start asking questions. If she did, he'd stonewall her. He didn't want to talk about his mother or his sister. And as for why his father wasn't there—he *definitely* wasn't talking about that. The man who'd made his childhood a misery; the man whose shadow still haunted him. None of the fear had gone away; it had just refocused. Dante wasn't scared any more that he'd be hurt; he was terrified that he'd be the one doing the hurting.

The silence between them stretched so long that it became painful.

And Dante was exceedingly relieved when his phone rang.

'Thanks, Mario.' He looked at her as he ended the call. 'Back in a second.'

The swordfish with lemon and oregano was perfect, the fresh vegetables were al dente, just as he liked them, and her eyes widened in appreciation at the white chocolate cheesecake. 'Wow. Your chef is brilliant. Please thank him—or her—for me.'

'Him. Sure.'

She sighed. 'You've gone all closed on me again.'

He shrugged. 'I'm your business mentor.'

And her lover.

But what was happening between them was nothing to do with love. It was just sex. Lust. Desire. She supposed he was right: she didn't need him to open up to her. This wasn't a relationship.

'All right. Your homework,' he said.

'Homework?'

'The next three days, you do a stint in every single job. Get to know the business. And then on Saturday you can tell me about your customers. Who they are, what they want, what your best-sellers are and why.'

'Got it.' She paused. 'So I don't see you until Saturday.'

'No.'

'Can I call you if I get stuck?'

He'd rather she didn't. He wanted a little distance between them. So he could get himself back into a more disciplined and controlled frame of mind. One where she didn't tempt him so much. 'If you absolutely have to. But I'd rather you called me with solutions than problems.'

'Got it.' She took a deep breath. 'Can I do the washing up?'

'Do you know how?' The question was out before he could stop it.

She looked hurt. 'I don't believe you sometimes, Dante. Why do you always have to think the worst of me?'

'I'm sorry.'

'You've got a chip on your shoulder a mile wide. I can't help that I was born into a rich family. Or that my grandparents spoiled me because I was all they had left of their own child.' Her eyes were suspiciously bright. 'Just so you know, I'd have given up all that privilege to have my parents back.'

'I'm sorry.' And now he felt really bad. He knew she'd lost her parents at the age of six. Tough for any child— though he would've been more than happy to have lost his own father at that age. Or even earlier.

Awkwardly, he pushed his chair back, walked over to her and wrapped his arms round her. 'I'm sorry, Caz.' It was the first time he'd used her name. The diminutive she'd asked him to use. And he knew she'd noticed, because she gave the tiniest shiver. 'I didn't mean to hurt you. And I don't have a chip on my shoulder.'

'Don't you?'

'No. Well, maybe a little,' he allowed. He pressed his mouth to her shoulder. 'I'd better take you home.'

'I'm perfectly capable of seeing myself home.'

'I know. But I'm Italian. And so are your grandparents. They're going to worry that you're late home.'

'Why?'

'Did you tell them you were seeing me?'

'No. Why would I tell them?' She frowned. 'I don't live with them, Dante.'

'You don't?' He was taken aback. He'd been so sure that she would've moved back in with her grandparents. Back to being spoiled.

'No. I live in the flat above my office.'

Like him.

Though he'd just bet that her flat was filled with fripperies. Cushions. Girly, princessy stuff. And he held himself in check: he didn't need to know what her flat was like. This wasn't going to be a relationship.

'OK. I know where it is.' He ushered her out of the kitchen, then slid his leather jacket round her shoulders. 'Better wear this.'

'Why? Doesn't your car have a roof, or something?'

'I don't have a car.'

She frowned, and then her eyes widened when he took her into the garage. 'A motorbike?'

'Top of the range, actually.' His one indulgence. 'And a bike's the most efficient form of transport through Naples. Why sit in a queue in a car, wasting time, when you can cut through it on one of these?'

'Good point.' Though she looked slightly nervous. 'I've never been on a motorbike.'

'It's OK. I'm a safe driver. Well. I am when I have a passenger,' he amended. 'On my own, I sometimes drive too fast.'

'Now there's a surprise,' she drawled.

He loved it when she was sassy with him, like this. And he almost, almost kissed her. But he held himself back, and instead handed her his spare motorbike helmet. 'The shoes aren't exactly what you should wear on a bike, but I can't do anything about that.'

She grinned. 'You love my shoes really.'

'Yeah, right.' He rolled his eyes. 'Put the jacket on properly.'

She did as he asked, and he climbed onto the bike. 'Get on behind me. And hold on,' he directed.

Dante Romano was full of surprises. Carenza would never have guessed that he had a motorbike. She'd expected him to have some kind of executive car. In dark grey. To go with his shark suit.

The bike was more of a bad boy thing. The bad boy in the leather jacket who'd taken her home, pinned her against the wall and kissed her stupid, before taking off all her clothes and making her burst into flames. The bad boy who'd gone all brooding on her. The bad boy whose washboard abs felt absolutely wonderful against her arms.

He was as good as his word, not taking it too fast as he drove her home.

And Carenza was sorry to give him back his jacket. Wearing it had felt like being held by him. Though that was crazy. She didn't need to be held by him. Didn't need a man in her life to make her feel worthwhile. She could stand on her own two feet. And she was going to make a success of her family business, really make everyone proud of her. Including herself.

'Do you want to come up for coffee?' she asked.

He shook his head. 'I have work to do. So have you.'

'Yeah. Homework.' She paused. 'You have to eat on Saturday, right?'

'Right.' He looked wary.

'Then let's save time and talk about my homework over dinner. I'll cook for us. It won't be up to your chef's standards, but I can boil water without burning it.'

He gave her a smile that made desire lick all the way up her spine. 'Said it before I could, hmm?'

'Something like that. Saturday, eight o'clock, here,' she said.

Was he going to kiss her goodnight?

Even the thought took her breath away.

But he didn't. He simply sketched a salute. 'Saturday, eight o'clock. *Ciao.*'

'Ciao,' she said, and watched him slide the jacket on and drive away.

Dante Romano was the most complex man she'd ever met. Half the time she wanted to slap him; the other half, she wanted to kiss him. He confused her and irritated her and—and he was so damn sexy that he made her bones melt.

But he'd made it very, very clear that as far as he was concerned this thing between them was just sex. That he could compartmentalise work and pleasure. And it looked as if she'd better learn to do the same.

CHAPTER FIVE

I'D RATHER you called me with solutions than problems.

Dante had expected at least one email, if not a phone call. But Carenza was absolutely silent until Saturday. And he was shocked to discover that he was disappointed. He'd actually wanted to hear her voice.

Oh, this was ridiculous. They weren't having a relationship, and he wasn't going to let himself get involved with her.

And yet he found himself emailing her. Just to make sure that he was still seeing her tonight.

Still OK for mentor meeting this evening?

Her reply was short—and very, very sassy.

8. Don't be late.

He couldn't help a grin. And he only just stopped himself emailing her back, to say, 'Or else…?'

Funny, he'd never sparred with previous girlfriends like this.

Not that Carenza was his girlfriend. What was happening between them was just sex. Scratching an itch for both of them.

Though he still enjoyed sparring with her. Yes, she was a princess—but he was starting to realise that there was more to her than that. And the more he discovered about her, the more he was starting to like her. She saw life from a very different angle from his own; although it annoyed him at times, it also intrigued him.

No, he wasn't finished with her yet. Not by a long way.

At exactly eight o'clock, there was a rap on the shop door. Carenza—who had sent her staff home early and had just finished tidying up the shop—let Dante in and locked the door behind him.

He was carrying a gorgeous confection of white roses and lilies. 'For you.'

'Dante, they're lovely. I wasn't expecting...' She buried her face in them. The scent was glorious. These weren't just any old flowers he'd picked up from a supermarket or market stall—these were seriously posh flowers. The kind you ordered from a florist.

He shrugged. 'It's usual to bring your hostess a gift when you're invited to dinner.'

Mmm, and he wouldn't be bringing wine, for obvious reasons. Which was probably why he'd gone so over the top with the flowers.

And she loved them.

'It's a business meeting,' she said. Just so he knew she didn't think this was a date.

He wasn't a shark in a suit, tonight. He wasn't dressed as a bad boy, either. He was something in between: black jeans, and a black cashmere sweater that made her itch to stroke it. Except that would lead to stroking his skin, and that would lead to kissing, and that would lead to...

Oh, she really had to stop letting her thoughts run away

with her. 'Come on up,' she said, and ushered him up to her flat.

At the top of the stairs, she kicked off her shoes. 'I'll just put these gorgeous flowers in water.'

He followed her into the kitchen. 'So how was your homework, Princess?'

So he was back to calling her that again, was he? And she had a pretty good idea why. 'You're right, doing all the jobs gave me more of an idea what my staff have to do.' She gave him a level stare. 'And, yes, I did clean the toilets.'

He laughed. 'Good. So you're not afraid of hard work.'

'I told you I wasn't.' She contented herself with a brief glower at him, and arranged the flowers in a vase. 'I'll just put these in the living room. Stay here—we're eating in here and my notes are in here.'

He looked faintly amused by her attempt at bossing him around, but he sat down at her kitchen table.

'Coffee?' she asked when she came back in.

'It depends if you're planning to spill it on me.'

She felt her skin heat. 'Trust you to bring that up. It was an accident. I was nervous.'

'And you're not now?'

'No.' After what they'd shared together, she wasn't nervous of him. There were times when he completely flummoxed her, but she wasn't nervous. He intrigued her. And she wanted to learn from him—as well as take him straight to her bed.

'Thank you, but I'll pass on the coffee. So, homework. You know your customers?'

She nodded. 'They're mainly families. The most popular flavours are vanilla, chocolate and strawberry, in that order—which is pretty much the same as it is in the rest of Europe. And vanilla's top in the States, too.' Just so he'd know she was looking at the big picture and was capable of doing her own research. 'And in my shops, they're closely followed by hazelnut, coffee, lemon and *stracciatella*.'

'I'm impressed. You know your product and you know your customers. So now you need to decide how you grow the business. Either you need to sell more things to your current customer base, or you need to increase your customer base.'

She frowned. 'Who buys ice cream, apart from families?'

He coughed. 'I thought I was supposed to be the one who asks the questions? Think about it.' He shrugged. 'Or think about *where* families buy ice cream.'

'From a *gelateria*, a stall or a kiosk...' She thought about it. 'Actually, one of my friends in London was a wedding planner. She did a summer wedding once with an ice cream cart for the guests, and apparently the kids absolutely loved it.'

He raised an eyebrow. 'London's a bit far to ship ice cream from Naples.'

'Very funny. I meant maybe I could offer something to local wedding planners. Maybe we could produce tubs to the bride and groom's specifications, with their name on it and the date of the wedding or something.'

'That's a good thought. Where else do you buy ice cream?'

He pushed her until she'd come up with a list including supermarkets, cinemas, hotels and restaurants. And although he was asking questions, he wasn't leading her—the ideas were all hers. He knew it, too, because he actually looked pleased. 'You're a quick learner and you can think on your feet. That's going to be good for Tonielli's.'

His praise warmed her. 'I'll research the openings, see where I can do some deals. The local deli, the cinemas...'

She paused. 'Or a restaurant chain. How about yours? Do you offer ice cream as a dessert?'

'I do.'

'Tonielli's?'

'Not at the moment.'

'But that's what you were planning.'

'What I planned is irrelevant, because you're running the business now.'

'So would you stock my ice cream in your restaurants?'

'That depends what you offer me.' He held his hand up to stop her talking. 'Don't rush into it, Princess—or into any other deal. You need to cost everything first and work out your strategy. I'll get you a marketing primer so you can work it out for yourself, then I'll go over the figures with you to see if I can add anything you haven't thought of. It's a bit of a conflict of interest, but between us we'll come up with something that's fair to both of us.'

'Thank you.' She smiled at him. 'Can we have a dinner break, now?'

'That'd be good.'

She walked over to the fridge. 'I did think about giving you nothing but ice cream.'

'Did you now?'

'I had a whole menu planned out. Tomato and basil sorbet, to start with. Like an iced soup.'

He sighed. 'If that's your idea of growing the business, I have to say it's an epic fail.'

'No, it was just a thought. But I couldn't come up with a reasonable flavour for the main course,' she admitted, 'except maybe parmesan, served on a waffle with salad, so I gave up on it.'

'Good. Because nothing but ice cream for dinner is just…' He grimaced. 'Well, it's too gimmicky. It wouldn't suit your customer base.'

'So you're telling me you've never eaten just ice cream for a meal?'

'No.' Dante pushed back the memories of the times when he'd had nothing at all for a meal. Because his father had drunk away the housekeeping budget yet again, and the local shopkeepers refused to give them credit because they knew his family was a bad risk.

'You're missing a trick. Having a duvet day and a tub of really good ice cream for lunch...'

'Is that an offer?' he drawled.

She backtracked fast. 'Time for dinner.' She took the plates she'd carefully arranged earlier from the fridge, a simple *tricolore* salad. 'And yes, I know this isn't proper cooking. It's just arranging things on a plate.'

He raised an eyebrow. 'You're defensive tonight, Princess.'

'That's because you make me defensive.'

He shrugged. 'Do you have something to be defensive about?'

How did he manage to wrongfoot her all the time? Just when she thought she knew what she was doing, every-thing shifted, and she found herself in the wrong. 'I guess not,' she muttered.

'It's good,' he said after the first mouthful. 'Fresh and simple, good quality ingredients, and nicely presented. It works for me.'

'Was that a compliment?'

He smiled. 'Don't push it, Princess.'

When they'd eaten the antipasti, she cooked some fresh pasta, drained it, and stirred in a simple pesto sauce. 'Go on, then. Ask me if I bought it from a shop,' she challenged when she put the plate in front of him.

He tasted it. 'No, this is definitely home-made.' The

lines round his eyes crinkled. 'Though I could ask you if your grandmother made it. Or her cook.'

She held out her left hand so he could see the plaster on her thumb. 'All my own work. See? I cut myself chopping the basil for the pesto.'

He took her hand and kissed her thumb. His mouth was warm and soothing, and at the same time it made her ache for him.

She sucked in a breath. 'What was that for?'

'Didn't you show me so I could kiss it better?'

Well, yes. Except whenever his mouth touched her skin, even if it wasn't overtly sexual, her body went into over-drive.

She managed to concentrate for long enough to serve up the simple chicken dish with vegetables for the main course, which he ate without comment—just an apprecia-tive smile.

And then she took the pudding from the freezer.

'Oh, now this is a definite cheat,' he said. 'Brought from downstairs, was it?'

'No. I'll have you know, I made this myself, this after-noon.' She paused. 'You know what you were saying about selling more products to the same customers? I'd already started to think about that and I was trying out a different idea.'

'Different?' His eyes narrowed. 'It looks like ordinary strawberry, to me.'

'Try it.'

He did. 'Strawberry. Though it's very light for ice cream.'

'I admit, it's a slight cheat—it's yoghurt-based. I didn't have time to make custard-based ice cream tonight,' she said.

'It's good. Very clean.'

'I wanted to appeal to customers who want all of the taste but less saturated fat in their diet.'

'That'd be good for the tourist market.'

Strange how his praise made her feel so good. 'I have plans for another, but that'll be at the opposite end of the spectrum. A custard-based one. Really rich. My favourite.' She licked her lower lip. 'Gianduja.'

'Chocolate.'

Cocoa butter and ground hazelnuts. 'Better-than-sex chocolate,' she corrected. 'And it drove me crazy that it was so hard to find in London. It's one of the nice things about coming home—you can buy gianduja everywhere.'

'Better-than-sex chocolate.' He looked at her thoughtfully. 'Is that a challenge, Princess?'

'What do you think?' She threw the question back at him.

He smiled. 'I think I'm going to buy some gianduja before I see you next. And then…' His eyes held the wickedest gleam. 'I'm going to make you beg.'

'In your dreams.'

He leaned across the table and kissed her. And even though only his mouth touched hers and he didn't so much as lay a finger on her, by the time he'd finished her knees were completely weak.

He didn't say a word to celebrate his triumph. He simply stroked her cheek with the backs of his fingers, as if to say that he knew this thing was bigger than both of them and it made him feel the same way. Upside down and inside out.

She dragged in a breath. 'Coffee? If I promise not to throw it over you?'

'That'd be lovely.' He nodded at the dirty pots and crockery stacked by the sink. 'Shall I sort that for you?'

'No, I'll do it later.'

'I don't mind.'

The idea of him being domesticated in her kitchen was a bit too much for her to handle. 'No. Go and sit in the living room. I'll bring coffee through.'

Dante couldn't just sit down and wait. And Carenza's living room was even more girly than he'd expected. Cushions. Lots of cushions. Ornaments everywhere, a mixture of the kitsch and the stylish. And the art on the walls was atrocious—brash abstracts that didn't even begin to tell him what they meant. Not his kind of thing at all.

There were photographs on the mantelpiece. OK, so it was prying—but she'd looked at his photos, so she could hardly complain if he followed her lead. He picked them up and studied them, one by one. Some were relatively recent, of herself with people he assumed were friends; there was one of herself with her grandparents that had obviously been taken at a family occasion, and another with them when she was really small. And the one that intrigued him most was of her with a younger couple, when she wasn't much more than a toddler.

'Are these your parents?' he asked when she walked in.

She nodded and set the tray of coffee down on the low table. 'I wish I'd had the chance to know them better. Everything Nonna, Nonno and my English grandparents told me about them—they were nice people. Kind. Good to be with.'

'What happened?' he asked softly.

'Car crash. Nonna and Nonno were looking after me for the weekend and my parents were going to celebrate their seventh wedding anniversary in Rome. A special treat, just the two of them—I mean, they loved me to bits, and I loved them, but time on your own with the love of your life is special.' She dragged in a breath. 'Except... They didn't come back.'

He could see that she was making an effort to hold the tears back, but one spilled over and dragged its way down her skin. He wiped it away with his thumb. 'Caz, don't cry.'

'You're using my name again.' Her voice was all shaky.

He stroked her hair back from her forehead. 'Don't read anything into it, Princess. And we're not getting involved with each other. I wouldn't be good for you.'

'How do you know?'

'I just do.' She'd want far more time than he'd be prepared to give her. She'd push him and push him—and if his control snapped, it would be a disaster.

She sighed. 'And now you're going to go all brooding again and shut me out.'

'Not everyone wants to bare their soul to the world.'

She nodded. 'That's a guy thing. I get it.'

'I'm sorry. I can't be who you need me to be.' He nuzzled her shoulder. 'One thing I can do for you, though.'

'Kiss it better?' she asked, her eyes huge and vulnerable and pleading.

This was a bad idea. He needed to stop this, right now. But his body wasn't listening to his head. 'Yes.'

Dante's mouth was warm and sweet and soothing; it felt like balm to her soul. As if he was trying to kiss the pain away.

She took his hand and led him to her bedroom.

His black cashmere sweater so soft under her fingertips, but better still was his skin when she'd peeled the sweater over his head. 'You're gorgeous,' she said, stroking his pectoral muscles. There was a light dusting of hair on his chest; she loved the friction against her fingertips.

'So are you.' He peeled off her strappy top and traced the lacy edge of her bra.

Her hand was shaking as she reached for the zip of his

jeans; he gave a sharp intake of breath as she eased the denim over his thighs.

It took him seconds to dispose of the rest of her clothes; then he carried her over to the bed, pushed the duvet aside and laid her against the pillows before climbing in next to her.

'You're such a princess,' he said, smiling as he sprawled on the mattress.

She knew exactly what he was talking about. 'Sheets with a high thread count are comfortable. What's so bad about that?'

'I knew your bed would be like this. Well, actually, no. I thought you'd have hundreds of cushions and this'd be a four-poster covered in voile.'

'Silk ribbons.' She curved her thumb and forefinger round his wrist.

'Is *that* what you're thinking, Princess?' He licked his lower lip and gave her a smouldering look that turned her to mush. 'I think I like how your mind works.'

She laughed. 'If I was still in the art business, I'd *so* commission a painting of you.'

He raised an eyebrow. 'What kind of painting might that be?'

'Naked. And for my eyes only,' she said.

'Good, because I think my mother would have a fit if there were naked paintings of me on display all over Naples—not to mention what your grandparents would say.'

'Well, the décor in Tonielli's does need a bit of updating,' she teased.

'Not with naked pictures of me, it doesn't.'

'It'd draw in a lot of female customers.'

'If that's on your business plan, I'm red-penning it already.'

'No. This is separate. Just you and me.'

The vulnerable, needy girl had gone, replaced by a sparky, funny woman he liked a lot. And making love with her was pure pleasure. Particularly when she insisted on taking the lead and straddled him.

'I like this. Great view,' he said, reaching up to play with her breasts.

'And I'm in charge.'

Only because he was letting her—and the expression in her eyes told him she knew it, too. But he was enjoying indulging her. He loved it when she lowered herself over him and began to move. And he seriously adored it when she kissed him hard, demanding a response and getting it.

Once he'd dealt with the condom and come back to her bedroom, he pulled his clothes on again.

'Don't tell me you're planning to go back to work now?'

He shrugged. 'You know me. Dull, boring businessman.'

She sighed. 'Dante, don't you ever give yourself a break?'

He didn't even need to think about it. 'No. Stay there; I'll see myself out. Your homework this week is a SWOT analysis. Strengths, weaknesses, opportunities, threats. The idea is to turn weaknesses into strengths—'

'—and threats into opportunities. Got it,' she finished dryly.

'Good. See you Saturday. My office, seven thirty. *Ciao.*'

And he walked out of her bedroom.

Before he could give in to the temptation of her unspoken offer to stay.

CHAPTER SIX

ON THE Monday afternoon, Carenza came back to her office with a pile of notes following a trip to a competitor's *gelateria*, to discover a book smack in the middle of her desk, with a note stuck to it. *More homework: analyse your sales for the last five years. What are the trends and why? Split it by outlet. Dante.* His handwriting was bold and spiky and confident, like the man himself. And she was so disappointed to realise that she'd missed him.

Ha. How pathetic was she? For all she knew, he could've sent the book over by courier.

She emailed him swiftly.

Thank you for the book. All homework in progress.

Though first she needed to get the sales figures. Broken down by outlet.

That was when she discovered that her grandfather didn't have everything on a computer spreadsheet, the way Amy always had at the gallery. Everything was in paper format only. Which left her with no choice; she was going to have to talk to Emilio Mancuso and ask him for the information.

He frowned when she called in to see him and made her

request. 'Why do you want to see the last five years' figures?'

'So I can see the trends.'

He shrugged. 'There's no need. I've looked after things for your grandfather for the last five years.' He paused, and gave her a significant look. 'Since he had his heart problems.'

Heart problems? What heart problems? Why didn't she know anything about this? Though the last thing she wanted was for Mancuso to think that she'd been kept in the dark, so she kept her worries under wraps. She'd talk to her grandmother about this later.

'I know sales have been down, but there's really nothing to worry about. It's just the recession, and everyone's in the same boat.' He gave her a smile that didn't reach his eyes. 'You don't need to worry your pretty little head about it, *carissima*.'

Darling? She wasn't his darling. And he'd just used the phrase that always made her see red. Her pretty little head, indeed. Why wouldn't men take her seriously? Was she going to have to dress in frumpy clothes, stop wearing make-up, dye her hair mouse-brown and scrape it back into a bun, and don a pair of thick glasses before anyone would notice that she did actually have a brain?

And why wouldn't he just give her the figures and let her see them for herself? 'Nonno's put me in charge, and I can't do my job unless I have all the facts,' she said, more rudely than she'd intended, but his attitude infuriated her. 'I can see you're busy, Signor Mancuso, and I'd hate to disturb you unnecessarily. Just tell me where the paperwork is and I'll find it for myself.'

He went a dull red. 'I already told you. You don't need to do this.'

Another refusal. Did he have something to hide? She

narrowed her eyes at him. 'If it's a problem for you, I could always ask Nonno.' And she had some other questions to ask her grandparents, too. Such as why they hadn't breathed a word about her grandfather's heart problems.

Tight-lipped, he took her through to a dusty-looking office, rummaged on a shelf and handed her several books.

'I hope you don't mind me taking these back to my own office.' Before he had a chance to say he did mind, she added, 'Of course, I'll take great care of them. And I'll return them personally when I've finished.' And she called a taxi to take her back to her office; no way was she going to ask him to help her get the books back to her place.

But when she looked closely at the figures, it seemed to be just as Mancuso said: sales were simply dropping, year on year. Maybe her instinctive dislike of him had been wrong. Maybe he had nothing to hide after all, and he was just fed up because Nonno had handed the reins over to her instead of letting him continue to run the business.

Though surely he realised that, if Nonno had sold the business, Dante Romano would've brought his own management team in—maybe even taken over the reins himself, at first? So this was pretty much the same thing.

Well, she'd make her peace with him later in the week. Right now, she had more important questions to ask.

She arrived at her grandparents' house that evening with flowers for her grandmother and some of the little marzipan fruits she knew her grandfather adored. After dinner, she insisted on helping her grandmother in the kitchen.

'Nonna, why didn't you tell me about Nonno's heart problems?' she asked softly.

Elena Tonielli looked flustered. 'I don't know what you're talking about, *tesoro*.'

'Emilio Mancuso told me today. The ones Nonno had

five years ago.' She couldn't help the hurt spilling out. 'The ones you didn't tell me a thing about.'

'You were in London, *cara*. You were happy. We weren't going to drag you back here.'

She bit her lip. Had her grandparents really thought that she'd need to be dragged home? 'Nonna, you surely can't think that you and Nonno would ever take second place in my life? If I'd known he was ill, I would've got on the first plane from London.'

'And disrupted your life. I know. But you were doing so well in London and we didn't want to worry you. Nonno's fine.'

So had Mancuso been lying to her? 'So are you saying Nonno *didn't* have heart problems?'

'He had chest pains, yes, but it was more of a scare than anything else.'

But it had happened five years ago, and she hadn't had a clue about it. 'Were you ever going to tell me?' she asked. Her grandmother's awkward expression told her the answer, and she closed her eyes. 'I wish I'd never left Naples. If I hadn't gone abroad, hadn't been so selfish and stayed away…I should've come back and taken over from Nonno years ago. Like Papa would've done.' They both heard the words she left unspoken: *had he lived*.

'We only wanted to see you happy, *tesoro*,' Elena said softly. 'It was right you should spread your wings and see a bit of the world. And you needed to meet the English side of your family. We'd been selfish in keeping you to ourselves. We should've sent you over before.'

Carenza swallowed hard. 'You weren't selfish. You took me in, you gave me a home, gave me everything I wanted.' They'd been in their fifties when her parents had died, and dealing with a young child on top of their own grief must've been such a strain on them.

'We took you in because we loved you. And having you meant—well, it meant we still had some of Pietro. We could see him in you as you grew up.'

'So Nonno's been ill for the last five years?'

'He was in hospital for less than a day,' Elena reassured her. 'They said it was angina and told him to take it easier, that's all, and to use a spray under his tongue if he ever gets any more pains in his chest.'

'Nonno, take it easy?' she scoffed.

'I didn't give him a choice,' Elena said dryly. 'I told him I'd already lost my son and I wasn't prepared to lose my husband. So he agreed to slow it down, delegate the business to Emilio until...'

'Until what?' Until she was ready to come home and take over?

Elena flapped her hand dismissively. 'Never mind. He's fine. Now, stop fussing or your grandfather will want to know what we're talking about.'

'And we don't want to worry him and give him chest pains.'

'Exactly.' Elena smiled. 'Emilio's been so good to us. He's done so much, never asked us for a thing.'

And now Carenza had waltzed in from London and been given the business that he'd spent the last five years looking after. No wonder he was hostile towards her: she was taking everything away from him and not giving him any credit for the work he'd put in. She made a mental note to make more of an effort with him.

'Now, let's go and join Nonno. And not too much business talk, please.'

'I'm doing a good job with the *gelateria*, Nonna. I'm not going to let Nonno down.'

'I know, *tesoro*. And it's good to have you home.'

* * *

Carenza spent the rest of the week working hard on the SWOT analysis Dante had asked for—and trying to be pleasant to Emilio Mancuso, though he didn't make it easy for her. And, even though she kept trying to remind herself of how much her grandparents valued him and how good he'd been to them, she still couldn't warm to the man. What it was about him, she didn't know, but there was definitely *something*. Or maybe she was just taking it out on him because her grandparents had leaned on him five years ago instead of on her, and she resented that.

She sighed. Why did it all have to be so complicated?

At half-past seven precisely on the Saturday, she knocked on the door of Dante's office.

'Coffee?' he asked.

She needed more than coffee. Right now, she thought, she could do with her body weight in chocolate. Probably intravenously. But coffee would have to do. 'Thank you.'

'So how's the SWOT analysis?' he asked.

'Getting there.' Though she'd found it hard to concentrate. Mancuso's revelation had shocked her and, although her grandmother had reassured her that Nonno was absolutely fine now, Carenza couldn't get it out of her head. 'Did you know my grandfather had heart problems, five years ago?'

He raised an eyebrow. 'No.'

'I would've come home, if I'd known.'

He frowned. 'Of course you would. That's obvious.'

She stared at his desk. 'My grandparents didn't even tell me he was ill.'

'They probably had their reasons.'

'Nonna told me. Because I was in London, I was happy, and they didn't want to disrupt my life.' She looked up at him. 'You're right about me. I *am* a princess. A spoiled, selfish bitch.'

'You're a princess and, yes, you've been spoiled,' he said softly, 'but you're not selfish. Well, not very,' he amended, 'considering your background. You're definitely not a bitch. And you forgot to add the good points.'

'Which are?'

'Fishing now, Princess?'

She lifted her chin. 'No.'

'No?'

She sighed. 'All right. It's been a horrible week, right now I don't like myself very much, and it'd be nice to have just a *little* bit of encouragement. People need carrots as well as sticks, you know, and a bit of praise can do wonders for someone's morale.'

'I'm glad you've worked that out.' He sat on the edge of the desk, his dark eyes glinting. 'OK. Your good points. You realised that you couldn't handle the business on your own and you had the sense to find yourself a mentor instead of wading in and getting into even more of a mess. You're not afraid of hard work. You're quick—I don't have to repeat myself—and you have real potential as a businesswoman because you can think outside the box. And you're starting to think about the people who work for you as people.' There was a teasing quirk to the corner of his mouth. 'And you wear very, very sexy shoes.'

She glowered at him. 'Which undercuts everything else you just said. Everything comes back to the way I look, the way I dress, and I *hate* that.'

He stroked her cheek. 'Don't be hard on yourself, Caz. That's my job.'

She gave him a wry smile. 'Yeah. You'll always tell me like it is. Sorry. I know you were just teasing me and trying to cheer me up. I'm being a cow.'

'You're really out of sorts, tonight.'

'And I didn't want to be, because Saturdays are the best day of the week.'

Because that was when she saw him? Although she didn't say it, it was written all over her face. And he needed to be fair to her. He couldn't let her rely on him, not emotionally. He didn't do emotional stuff. 'This isn't a relationship, Princess,' he warned softly.

'I know. It's about business.'

She sounded so disgruntled that he couldn't help smiling. 'Are you saying Saturdays aren't enough for you?'

'No, I have to resort to—' She clapped a hand over her mouth, flushing. 'Forget it.'

When she'd just been on the verge of confessing something interesting? Right now, she had his full attention. 'Tell me what you were going to say, Princess.'

'No.'

Her face was so expressive that he could guess exactly what was going through her head. And maybe this would take her mind off her worries. It certainly took his mind off everything else, when he was with her. He moved closer. 'You have to resort to what?'

'Nothing.'

He took her hands and pulled her to her feet, before whispering in her ear, 'Carenza Tonielli, are you trying to tell me that some nights you think of me and you touch yourself?'

If she'd blushed before, that was nothing compared to now. Her face was like a beacon.

Except what had started out as teasing had suddenly turned into something else. Something that made it hard for him to breathe. It felt as if someone had just dumped him on top of Vesuvius.

'Show me,' he said.

She looked horrified. 'I can't do that in front of you!'

Oh, yes, she could—and he'd enjoy every single second of it. 'Then pretend I'm not here.' He stole a kiss. 'Show me.' It was a request, not a command. Tempting her, the way she tempted him.

'No.'

But her voice was deeper. Huskier. Filled with the same desire he felt.

Right now, he was pretty sure they both needed this.

He took her hand, drew her middle finger into his mouth and sucked hard. Her pupils dilated and it looked as if she, too, were having problems breathing.

But he could guess why she'd gone shy on him. This was his office. Anyone could walk in. And this was something for his eyes only.

'Let me make it easier for you,' he said. He strode over to lock his office door and draw the blinds.

She bit her lip. 'I know you know about...'

Her wild past. In a different country. Where nothing would get back to her grandparents. 'Yes,' he said softly.

'But I've never...' She shook her head.

And suddenly he knew why she was holding back. 'You're not a tart, Caz,' he said, keeping his voice gentle. 'You're a beautiful, incredibly sexy woman, and I love the fact that you're so responsive to me.'

'You think I'm so uninhibited, I'd put on a show for you.' She looked close to tears.

'No.' He drew her close. 'It's a guy thing. I love the idea that you touch yourself and think of me when I'm not with you. And right now I'm as turned on as hell.' He shifted so that she could feel the evidence for herself. 'I've got all these pictures in my head. Except they're not enough. Not when you're here with me. I want to see you for myself.'

He brushed a kiss against her mouth. 'If it makes you feel any better, I've had to resort to my own right hand, too.'

'You touch yourself and think of me?' she whispered.

'Yeah.' His voice sounded rusty as he confessed to her. 'Since you ask, in the shower, this morning.' He paused. 'And not just this morning, either.'

She looked shocked for a moment—and then more than a little pleased.

'See? You're thinking the same thing, now.'

'I… Yes,' she admitted.

'This is just between you and me.' He caught her lower lip between his. 'I want you naked. And, yeah, I want you uninhibited. Not because I think you're easy, but because I think you're the most sensual woman I've ever met. And nobody's ever turned me on as much as you do.'

She said nothing, but she made no protest when he peeled off her strappy top and dropped it on the floor next to her. Or when he unzipped her jeans and pushed the soft denim over her hips, easing her jeans down until they pooled at her feet. Wearing only her bra and knickers, she stood before him.

'You're gorgeous,' he said, and stole another kiss. 'So will you show me what happens when you imagine me touching you?'

She closed her eyes. For a moment, he thought she was going to refuse—and then she slid one hand between her legs. Slowly, almost shyly, she leaned back against his desk and began to stroke herself.

Dante lasted a minute, if that, before dropping to his knees in front of her, ripping off the lacy confection of her knickers—because they were in the way and he couldn't wait to take them off properly—and copying the movements of her hand with his tongue.

She whimpered and slid her hands into his hair, urging him on.

He teased her clitoris with the tip of his tongue, until he felt her knees buckle slightly. He pushed a finger inside her, gratified when she rocked her pelvis against him to draw him deeper. And then he teased her clitoris a bit more, feeling her tighten round him with every stroke of his tongue. When he felt her shudder, he drew her clitoris into his mouth and sucked. Hard.

'Dante.' His name was a tortured whisper—and he felt the convulsions rip through her. He waited until the aftershocks had died down, then straightened up.

'You look pleased with yourself,' she said, her tone waspish.

Probably because he was still fully clothed and she was wearing one tiny bit of lace, and she was embarrassed to have lost her control completely under his touch. He grinned. 'Of course I'm pleased with myself. You just came in my mouth.'

'Dante!' Again, her face turned beetroot.

He laughed. 'I love this side of you, Caz—when you try to be a bad girl.'

She narrowed her eyes at him. 'What do you mean, *try*?'

'Because you're not a bad girl.'

'Even though—'

'Forget about London. It doesn't matter. It's not who you are.' He stroked her cheek. 'And you're so gorgeous, you drive me a little bit crazy.' He dragged in a breath. 'I've never asked anyone to do what I just asked you to do.'

It sent a thrill through Carenza, to discover that she could distract this incredibly focused man enough to make him act out of character.

And he clearly wanted her as badly as she wanted him.

She licked her lower lip. 'Once a week isn't enough.'

'I know. It's not enough for me, either.' He gave her a hard, intense look. 'But I still can't offer you a relationship.'

'I get that. I'm not going to start stamping my foot or demanding things.'

'Good.' He smiled. 'I bought something today. Something I think you'll like.'

Her heart skipped a beat. 'I'm not sure if I dare ask.'

'You gave me a challenge, last week.'

'Did I?'

'Yeah.' He gave her the most sinful smile. 'Come upstairs with me.'

'No way am I walking out of your office practically naked.' She scooped up her clothes, intending to pull them on again—and then she realised what she'd been too carried away to notice before. 'You ripped my knickers, Dante.' And now they were completely unwearable.

'Um, yeah. Sorry.' Though he didn't exactly look repentant. 'I got impatient.'

'Which means I have to spend the rest of the evening with no underwear.'

'That works for me, Princess.' He brushed a swift kiss against her mouth. 'But I'll buy you some new knickers to replace them, OK?'

She closed her eyes. 'You're really, *really* good at embarrassing me. And you don't have to buy me underwear.'

'Don't be embarrassed. I enjoyed every second of what we just did.' He moved closer. 'Feel what you did to me.'

She could. And breathing was a problem again. 'Uh.'

'And I love it when I can silence you like that.' He stole a kiss. 'Come on.'

She dressed swiftly; he unlocked his office door, then

locked it again behind them before letting them into his flat and leading her into his kitchen.

'Close your eyes, Princess,' he said.

'Why?'

'Because I'm asking you to.' He gave her a lazy smile. 'This is going to be fun. I promise. Trust me.'

Did she trust him? Well—yes. Otherwise that encounter in his office just now wouldn't have happened. She knew he wasn't going to gossip about her or make her feel bad. When she was with him, she didn't have to worry about anything.

She closed her eyes; a moment later, she could feel something brushing against her lower lip.

'Keep your eyes closed,' he whispered. 'Open your mouth.'

She couldn't help doing what he asked.

'Now bite.'

Her mouth was flooded with the taste of gianduja, the rich mixture of ground hazelnuts and cocoa butter that she'd loved since childhood.

'Good?' he asked, his voice husky.

'Very.'

'Better than sex, you said.'

She opened her eyes and looked at him.

'I think I'm going to enjoy making you take that back.' This time, his smile was positively wolfish.

It took him less than ten minutes to have her babbling that yes—oh, God, *yes*—sex with him was better than chocolate. And then he made her admit it all over again.

'Good. Just so we're clear on that,' he said, when her third climax of the evening had died away.

He disappeared, then returned with two mugs of coffee. 'Right. Time to tackle the SWOT analysis.'

'Uh.' She swallowed hard. 'How the hell do you expect me to concentrate on business, when you just wiped every single thought out of my head?'

'That's what the coffee's for, Princess.'

She blew out a breath. 'You amaze me.'

He kissed her swiftly. 'I'll take that as a compliment. Even though I think it was a backhanded one. Now, focus. I want to see those notes.'

As before, Dante took Carenza home on the bike and refused to come in for coffee, saying that he had things to sort out.

But, the next day, she was gratified to discover an email from him in her inbox.

How about a mentoring session on Wednesdays as well?

He didn't mean just mentoring, she knew that. Not after what had happened between them last night.

And the fact that he wanted to see her, too...

Dante had made his position clear enough, the previous night. *I still can't offer you a relationship.* But Carenza had a feeling that he was definitely protesting too much. His head might be able to come up with a dozen or more reasons why he shouldn't have a relationship with her, but his body told her another story. And maybe she could teach him that you didn't always have to listen to your head. That there was nothing wrong with letting yourself get close to someone—that it was OK to be attracted to someone and to act on that attraction. And it was OK to lose control. Twice, now, she'd stripped for him while he'd been fully clothed and in full control throughout. It was time she evened up the balance.

Maybe, she thought, she could mentor him. Teach him to let go and have some fun.

Maybe.

CHAPTER SEVEN

By Wednesday, Carenza wasn't any further forward with the sales figures. 'I can't get them to work,' she told Dante over a pizza that evening. 'Though I'm not stupid.'

He rolled his eyes. 'Of course you're not.'

'I really can't understand *why* they're down. All I can tell you is that they're slowing, year on year. Signor Mancuso says it's because we're in a recession.'

'Right. And the definition of profit is?'

'Sales minus costs.'

'Exactly. So if you can't increase your sales to increase your profits, then you need to cut your costs,' he said.

'Are you suggesting I should get rid of some of the staff?' She sucked in a breath. 'I can't do that, Dante. How are they going to pay their bills if they don't have their job any more?'

'Staff aren't your only costs,' he pointed out. 'And remember that your staff are assets, too. You need to look at your variable costs.'

'The ones that change with the volume of sales,' she said.

He smiled. 'You've been paying attention. Good. So what can you tell me about your raw materials?'

'We've been making ice cream in Naples for more than a hundred years—and we've always used organic produce.

Only the best. We've used the same suppliers for years and years and years,' Carenza said. 'Nonno says if you don't use the best, you can't produce the best.'

'Years and years and years, hmm? That sounds like a rut to me. You always need to audit your suppliers every so often and check that they're still giving you the best value for money,' Dante said. 'Just because they've been the best in the past, it doesn't mean they're the best now. New people come along with new ideas and new technologies, and things change.'

'So I sack my suppliers, even though we go way back?' She bit her lip. 'That feels a bit—well, ruthless.'

'I'm not saying you have to replace them. I'm saying you need to audit them and find out if they can do you a better deal than they're offering now. It's standard business practice. The way your figures are going,' he said softly, 'you'll be out of business within a year. And that means you'll have to let all your staff go.'

'But surely it's just the recession, and everything will be OK once the economy's back to normal?'

'You're in the same market as I am. Not a competitor, because you're in a different segment,' he reminded her, 'but my restaurants aren't facing the same problems you are, so it's not just the recession. Look at your costs, Princess. Are there other organic suppliers that can give you better deals?'

'So I just ring them up and say, hi, I'm Carenza Tonielli, give me a quote?'

'Yup.' He looked at her. 'Tell me who you use now. I'll ask them for a quote—and then you can compare that to what they offer you. That and the competitor quotes will help you drive their price down to a more reasonable level, if you want to keep using them.'

'But they have to make money, too.'

'Agreed—but, right now, my guess is they're making a little too much out of you. Time to get some balance back.'

'Thank you, Dante. I really do appreciate your help.'

He shrugged. '*Prego*, Princess.'

She was sure he called her that purely to annoy her. Though in a strange kind of way it was becoming an endearment. There wasn't an edge to his voice any more when he called her 'Princess'. There was something else. Something she couldn't quite define, but something she hoped might just grow.

For pudding, she'd organised something special.

'Is this another of your experiments?' he asked as she delved in the freezer.

She laughed. 'Yes. But you'll like this one. I promise it's not parmesan. Though I bet that parmesan ice cream would do well in a trendy London restaurant.'

'Where they care more about the presentation than the taste?' He grimaced. 'This is Naples, Princess. That means substance over style.'

She fished a spoon out of the drawer, and unclipped the lid from the plastic tub.

'Chocolate,' he said as soon as he saw the ice cream.

'Better-than-sex chocolate,' she corrected, feeding him a spoonful.

'Nope. It's good, but it's not that good.' He gave her a speculative look. 'Or maybe we should take this to bed, so I can compare them side by side…'

'You are *not* getting gianduja ice cream all over my sheets,' she said. 'I'll never get the marks out.'

He laughed. 'You're such a princess. Do you even do your own laundry?'

Her answer was to drop a spoonful of ice cream down the neck of his shirt.

'Oh, now that was a severely bad move, Princess.'

It took him thirty seconds to get them both naked on her kitchen floor.

Ten more to smear her with ice cream.

And rather a lot longer to lick it off. By the time he'd finished, Carenza was sated and smiling.

'I think we've established that the ice cream—good as it is—is still second best. You can't bill it as "better than sex" ice cream on your menu,' he teased.

'Uh. Let me get some brain cells back before I have to answer you,' she groaned. 'And I'm still sticky.'

'You started it,' he pointed out.

And she'd enjoyed every second of it. She loved it when Dante stopped being serious and became her teasing, exuberant lover. And she wanted more of this. Much more. 'I need a shower.' She licked a smear of ice cream from his abdomen. 'So do you.'

'Is that an offer?'

'Might be.' She gave him her sexiest pout. 'Interested?'

His answer was to pick her up and carry her to the shower. She'd run out of hot water by the time they'd finished, but she didn't care. The smile on her face felt a mile wide.

Wrapped in towels to keep off the chill, they lounged on her bed. And there was a softness in Dante's eyes that tempted Carenza to try to get him to open up to her. To start her private reverse mentoring.

'So what does a restaurateur do for fun,' she asked, 'given that he doesn't own a games console or TV?'

He grimaced. 'Most TV is pretty mindless—and I hate that reality stuff. Who wants to watch that tedious rubbish?'

'Not all TV's like that,' she said. 'There are documentaries. Comedies.' She paused. 'Do you like films?

He shrugged. 'My business takes up most of my time.'

'All work and no play,' she said, batting her eyelashes at him.

'Are you calling me dull, Princess?'

'No, you're not dull.' He had far too much energy to be dull. 'But maybe,' she said carefully, 'you're missing out on things.'

'So what do you do for fun?' he asked.

Was he being polite, or was he really interested? She wasn't sure. 'I haven't really had a chance to go out much since I've been back in Naples. But in London I used go to the cinema a lot,' she said. 'And I'd have a glass of wine afterwards with my friends so we could talk about the film.'

'Serious arty discussions, hmm?' His expression told her that he thought it was more likely that she was discussing the hunkiness of the male leads with her girly friends.

She folded her arms. 'If you call me an airhead again, I'll...I'll...'

'Yes?' He looked interested.

She subsided. 'Sometimes, Dante, you're so difficult.'

'And you're not?' he asked dryly.

'Not as difficult as you are, no.'

'So you like talking about films.' He rolled his eyes. 'Next you're going to tell me you're in a book group.'

'No, I'm not. But I do like reading.' She paused. 'You?'

'I read the business news. Usually online.'

She was still no closer to finding out how he let off steam. 'OK, I give up. What do you do for fun?'

'Sometimes I go out on the bike.'

'And that's *it*?'

He leaned closer. 'And sometimes I have sex with a gorgeous blonde. Fairly incredible sex, actually.'

She could feel her face going beetroot, and he spread his hands and laughed. 'Hey. Don't complain. You asked.'

'So I'm your main leisure activity?'

'At the moment, I guess so.'

She frowned. 'You don't ever go dancing?'

'Do I look like a man who dances?'

He looked like the kind of man who'd dance an incredibly sexy tango, one that would leave her wet and panting for him. Not that she was going to tell him that. 'Let's give it a try. Will you go out with me on Saturday night?'

'Dancing? Sorry, Princess, not my scene.'

'How do you know? You've never been dancing with me. It'll be fun.' She tipped her head to one side and gave him her most winsome smile. 'Come with me.'

'I'd rather not.' He pulled a face. 'I hate dancing.'

She sighed. 'You're the one who says we don't understand each other. If you come with me, see what I do for fun, then maybe you'll understand a bit better what makes me tick.'

'I understand you already.'

'No, you don't. You just think you do. The same as I know that whenever I think I've worked you out, I'm going to find out there's yet another layer.'

'Now you're calling me an onion?'

'No. Just complex.' She kissed him lightly. 'Come with me, Dante. We'll have a good time. If you really hate it, we don't have to stay.' She gave him her sexiest pout. 'Don't you want to get hot and sweaty with me?'

'I can think of better ways,' he said.

'Trust me, it'll be a lot more fun than you think.' She licked her lower lip. 'I guarantee you'll like my dress. And my shoes.' She could see in his face that he was looking for excuses. 'Saturday night is mentor night,' she reminded him. 'Only, this time, I'll be mentoring you.'

He frowned. 'How do you mean?'

'I'm mentoring you in having fun. In understanding me. In what makes me tick.'

Dante thought about it. He didn't need to know what made her tick. That was nothing to do with the mentoring arrangement—or the fact they still couldn't be in the same room as each other for long without needing to rip each other's clothes off. But he still didn't want any emotional involvement. Still couldn't handle it.

'Please, Dante. I've been working really hard. I'd like an evening off.' She paused. 'And you work harder than I do.'

He shrugged at the implication. 'I don't need time off.'

'Just an hour. That's all,' she said. 'Please?'

It was hard to resist the appeal in those blue, blue eyes. He sighed. 'This is against my better judgement,' he said, 'but OK. Not this Saturday—next week.'

It was a compromise. And she'd take it. 'Thank you.' She slid her arms round him and held him close. 'I promise you won't regret it.'

'So how did you get on with the figures?' Dante asked on the Saturday night.

'I'm still waiting for some of the quotes. But I did look at the variable costs.' She paused. 'And something's wrong there.'

'Come and sit down, and we'll take a look at it.' He drew another chair round to his side of the desk.

'If I'm selling less ice cream, that means I don't have to make so much of it in the first place, so I should be using fewer ingredients—right?'

'That should be how it works, yes.'

'But I'm not. If anything, according to the invoices, I'm using more.'

He frowned. 'Are you sure?'

She nodded. 'And I can't see a reason for it. I don't want to worry Nonno in case it sets off his angina. I guess I should ask Emilio Mancuso, seeing as he's been manager for the last five years.' She sighed. 'The last time I asked him something, he told me not to worry my pretty little head about it.'

'What an idiot.' Dante gave her a wry smile. 'Did you accidentally-on-purpose stand on his foot—in your sharpest heels?'

'I wanted to,' she admitted, 'but I resisted the impulse. I can see why he doesn't like me. He's been running everything for five years, then I waltz in from London and take over, when I know next to nothing about the business. It's kind of a slap in the face to him, and I need to take his feelings into consideration when I deal with him.'

'Understanding your staff always helps.' Dante raised an eyebrow. 'But he doesn't know you at all, does he?'

She frowned. 'What makes you say that?'

'Because if he did, he'd realise you're here to stay. So he should be working with you and making himself your right-hand man, instead of putting obstacles in your way. Mentoring you to make sure all the work he's put in isn't all undone.'

She grimaced. 'I already told you, I couldn't ask him to be my mentor.'

'Because you don't trust him?'

'I don't know. I can't put my finger on it, but there's something about him. Whether it's the fact he resents me for swanning in, or I resent him for being there for my grandparents when I should've been there…I don't know. And I feel so bad saying that.' She sighed. 'I don't know what to do, Dante. And I hate that.'

'Bide your time,' he said. 'Don't rush into anything. Gather all your facts, first, look at them, and then you can make an informed decision. But don't rush it.'

CHAPTER EIGHT

On Tuesday morning, Carenza was working through a set of figures when an unexpected visitor arrived.

'Nonno!' She threw her arms round her grandfather. 'Come and sit down.'

It felt slightly odd to be the one behind the desk she'd visited her grandfather sitting at during her childhood, but he didn't seem to mind.

'I see you've made changes to the artwork in the office,' Gino said with a smile.

'It's one of the three pictures I brought back from Amy's. The other two are upstairs in my flat.'

'It's…' He was clearly searching for a diplomatic word. 'Bright.'

Dante had been much less tactful in his reaction. Especially when she'd suggested using prints of the artist's work in the shops and the ice cream *caffè*.

'Sorry, Nonno. It's your office. I shouldn't be making changes.' She bit her lip.

'*Tesoro*, it's your office now. You arrange it however you like.' Though there was a slight trace of worry in his voice when he asked, 'Is that what you had in mind when you said you were changing the pictures on the walls in the shops?'

Not after Dante's comments, it wasn't. 'No. But we've been here for over a hundred years. It's our USP, really, that I'm the fifth generation of Toniellis to run the shops. So I thought it might be nice for our customers to see photographs of how things used to be when the business first started.'

Gino looked pleased. 'That's a good idea.'

'So I thought maybe you, Nonna and I could look through all the old photos, some time soon, and pick the ones we like best. Starting with your great-grandfather.' She paused. 'And including Papa.'

'Including Pietro.' There was a suspicious sheen in his eyes. She knew exactly how he felt. Every time she thought of her parents, it made her catch her breath and her eyes feel moist, too. Ridiculous, after all this time. She'd spent much more of her life without them than with them. Three-quarters of it, if you were counting. But she still missed them.

'Can I get you some coffee, Nonno?'

'That would be lovely, *piccola*.'

She made coffee for both of them, and retrieved a tin of cannoli wafers filled with chocolate-hazelnut spread from the bottom drawer of her desk. 'My secret vice. Help yourself.'

'Thank you. So how are you getting on, *tesoro*?' Gino asked.

'Fine. I'm enjoying it.'

'Emilio tells me you've been asking him lots of questions.'

There was a slight edge to her grandfather's tone—something she'd never known before—and it put her on full alert. Was Mancuso trying to make trouble between them? 'Well, I guess I have—I've been trying to get to know the business properly. If I've been a nuisance, then I'm sorry. I'll try not to bother him so much in future.'

'It's not that.' Gino paused. 'He feels you don't trust him.'

Help. How did she answer that?

Obviously her expression did it for her, because her grandfather sighed. 'Emilio's a good man, Carenza. He's looked after the business for the last five years, been my right-hand man for many years more than that. He doesn't deserve to be treated like this.'

Carenza wasn't so sure, but she had no proof to back up her feelings. And a hunch wasn't enough.

Dante's voice echoed in her head. *Gather all your facts, first.*

As if her grandfather could read her mind, he said, 'I hear you've been seeing Dante Romano.'

'He's my business mentor,' she explained. Her grandfather didn't need to know the rest of it.

'You do know he wanted to buy the business?'

'Yes, which makes him the best person I could ask.' She gave an expressive shrug. 'You know what they say. Keep your friends close, and your enemies even closer.' Not that Dante was her enemy. Even when they didn't see eye to eye.

Gino raised an eyebrow. 'Be careful, *tesoro*.'

'You're warning me off him?'

'Not in business. Dante's as straight as they come. But don't lose your heart to him. As soon as he sees wedding bells in a girlfriend's eyes, he leaves her.'

'I'm not his girlfriend.' And she certainly wasn't telling her grandfather about *that* side of her relationship with Dante. That was just between her and Dante.

'Just be careful. And don't break his heart, either.'

She looked at him, hurt. 'How do you mean?'

'You're not one to settle.'

Did he know about what had happened in London, last year? she wondered. If Dante knew, anyone else could find out, too, and tell her grandfather. Not Dante—she knew he'd never undermine her like that. But if Mancuso had any idea... Playing for time, she said, 'I don't understand, Nonno.'

'It'd be easy for a man to lose his heart to you, *tesoro*. You're sweet and you're beautiful,' he said. 'But you're twenty-eight years old and you still haven't found the man you want to settle down with. And Dante Romano had a rough time, as a kid.'

That didn't surprise her. It would explain why he was so self-contained, why he didn't let people close. And yet she knew he was close to his mother and his sister. 'What do you mean by "a rough time", Nonno?'

Gino shook his head. 'It's not for me to talk about.'

And she was pretty sure that Dante wouldn't tell her. 'He said you gave him a chance, when he was younger,' she said.

'I gave him a job.' Gino flapped his hand dismissively.

'I get the impression it was more than that.'

'And a little advice when he bought the first restaurant.'

'Exactly. He feels he owes you. That's why he's mentoring me.'

'Hmm. Well, just be careful,' Gino said.

Carenza was still seething about the way Emilio Mancuso had gone to her grandfather behind her back when she called in at Dante's office for her mentoring session on Wednesday evening.

He took one look at her. 'I'm feeding you first. You need carbs.'

'I'm fine.'

'No, you're not. Trust me to order for you?'

'Anything except clams.' She pulled a face.

'That's a shame, because Mario's been experimenting with pasta *vongole*—it has a chilli kick and it's seriously good.'

'*Really* not clams, please,' she repeated.

Rosemary bread and olives helped settle her temper; the pasta Alfredo, followed by a rich beef stew with tiny new potatoes and steamed mangetout, helped even more.

And then Dante gave her ice cream.

She tasted it gingerly. 'Not as good as mine,' she said, though she finished the bowl—the sugar rush was just what she needed to get rid of the last bit of her bad mood. 'I think you need to change your supplier.'

'Do you have anyone in mind?'

He was teasing her, and she knew it. She smiled. 'I might do.'

'Give me a quote, and we'll talk about it.' His smile faded. 'Talking of quotations—I heard back from your supplier.'

'And?'

Without comment, Dante cleared away the plates, then placed the quotation in front of her.

She stared at it. 'But—that's an awful lot less than they're charging me.'

'I thought it might be,' he said.

'Is this why my business is going downhill? This is what you thought when you said it was more than just the recession?'

'It's one of the reasons,' he said. 'But what's really worrying me is what you told me on Saturday—that your input is going up when your output is going down. It's not as if your business is something like a bakery, where you have to throw out unsold bread and pastries because they're stale, or sandwich shops where you have to get rid of the fillings because they're perishable and food hygiene rules demand it. By definition, *gelati*'s frozen. It doesn't go off from one day to the next. Unless you have a freezer breakdown—when you'd be throwing out everything and your losses would be insured in any case—there's no reason why you should throw the leftover *gelati* away each day. And I'm pretty sure you don't.'

She absorbed his words—and what he hadn't said explicitly really shocked her. 'You think someone's *cheating* us?'

He was silent.

'Mancuso?'

'I don't know.'

'But why? How?'

He spread his hands. 'At this stage, it's only a suspicion. I don't have the proof to back it up. But I'd advise you to take a close look at your business processes. When the ingredients are delivered, who checks them in and checks against the invoices that everything's there?'

'I'm not sure. So you think there might be fake invoices? Or Mancuso's ordering more ingredients than he should, then taking the excess and selling it on elsewhere?'

'Either of them is a possibility. And, when the ice cream's made, how do you know where it goes?'

'I don't know. And I *should* know.' She shook her head in disbelief. 'I hate the thought that he's doing this. Nonno trusts him.'

'You don't know for sure it's him—and you can't accuse him without having the facts.'

'So it could be someone else in the business?' She bit her lip. 'Did you know Nonno gives all the staff an extra week's wages at Christmas? And he does it at the end of November, so they have enough time to go out and buy

Christmas presents and what have you.' She sighed. 'And most of the staff have been there for *years*. I hate thinking that I can't trust anyone.'

'Trust no one. It's a pretty good business rule.'

She shook her head. 'No, it's not. It's cynical and horrible.'

'You're being naïve, Caz.'

She rested her elbows on the table and put her face in her hands. 'I can't take this in. And how the hell am I going to tell Nonno?'

'Wait until you have proof of who it is and what they're doing. Then you can decide what to do next.'

'God, this is such a mess. And you know I was looking at the invoices and what have you? Mancuso went to Nonno and complained about me—he says that I don't trust him.'

'Well, you don't,' Dante pointed out. 'I take it Gino wasn't happy about it?'

'No. He actually came down to the shop to see me, yesterday, and told me that Mancuso deserves better.' He'd warned her off Dante, too—not that she was going to tell him that.

'Better tread carefully, Princess.'

'"One may smile, and smile, and be a villain,"' she quoted bitterly.

'So you really think Mancuso's at the bottom of this?'

'I don't know. Part of me thinks he's resentful because he feels he should've stayed as manager and I should just be a—well, a figurehead, someone who clip-clops around in designer heels.'

He stole a kiss. 'You have to admit, you *do* do that.'

'But there's more to me than just my shoes. I don't want to be a figurehead. I want to run Tonielli's properly. And I want people to take me *seriously*.' She sighed. 'I guess I'm just going to have to make my peace with Emilio Mancuso. Somehow.'

'Like I told you before, don't rush into anything,' he advised. 'Be polite. And stay wary.'

Like Dante was, himself? she wondered. 'Are you still going dancing with me on Saturday?'

He gave her a pained look, as if he hoped she'd forgotten about it. 'I guess so.'

'Good. Because, right now, I think I need that.'

He raised an eyebrow. 'I know a very good way of releasing tension.'

'Yeah.' Except she knew he wasn't going to let her cuddle up to him afterwards. Or let her spend the night. And she needed to think things through: how she was going to persuade Dante to let this thing between them grow. From where she was standing, she thought it had potential. Huge potential. But he was stubborn, and until she could work out why he was so resistant to any kind of relationship, she was going to back off.

Temporarily.

Didn't they say that absence made the heart grow fonder? Maybe abstinence would do the same. 'I'd better leave you in peace. I'll see you on Saturday.' She kissed him briefly. *'Ciao.'* And then she left, before her hormones weakened her resolve and she let him carry her to bed.

Carenza had hoped that she'd given Dante time to think about them. But over the next couple of days she had a nasty feeling that she'd overplayed her hand and he was having second thoughts. Especially about going dancing with her on Saturday night. Maybe dropping into his office unannounced with a box of gianduja, with some trumped-up query, might give her the chance to remind him that she was doing the mentoring, next session.

When she got to the restaurant, the manager told her that Dante wasn't there. 'But Signora Ricci may be able to help you,' he said.

Dante's secretary, Carenza presumed. He certainly hadn't mentioned her; and Carenza had never been to his office in conventional business hours, so of course she wouldn't know any of his staff. And Dante Romano was the kind of man who gave information on a need-to-know basis. He'd obviously decided that she didn't need to know anything about his secretary.

Hesitantly, she rapped on the door. 'Signora Ricci?'

The woman sitting at the desk was in her early forties and perfectly groomed. Carenza had a feeling that she might turn out to be the dragon secretary type, who'd protect her boss from every interruption.

Signora Ricci looked up from her desk. 'Can I help you?'

'I was looking for Dante.'

'I'm afraid he's not here. I can take a message, if you wish.'

'It's OK. I'll email him.' She paused. 'But I did bring him this.' She handed the foil-covered box to Signora Ricci.

'May I say who left it?'

'I'm sorry, forgive my manners. I'm Carenza Tonielli. His, um—mentee, I guess.'

'Ah. *You're* Carenza.'

Dante had talked to his secretary about her? What had he said?

She blew out a breath. 'I know I'm taking up too much of his time. I just brought him some gianduja to say thank you for all the help he's been giving me. It isn't nearly enough, but...' She spread her hands. 'You can hardly send a man flowers, and taking him out to dinner, when he owns a chain of restaurants, feels a bit...well...*wrong*.'

Signora Ricci nodded.

Was that a slight softening in her face, or was it just wishful thinking? Carenza decided to take a chance. 'Actually, you might be the person to help me. Have you worked for him for very long?'

'About eight years. Why?'

'Because I've known him for a month now and I still don't have a clue what he likes—I don't even know what kind of music he listens to. I know he's my mentor and this is strictly business, but by now surely I should know more of what makes him tick?'

'Not necessarily. He keeps himself very much to himself,' Signora Ricci said.

And getting information out of him was like pulling teeth. 'I want to do something nice for him, but I don't know what. Maybe take him out somewhere nice.' Carenza wrinkled her nose. 'But he hates films, so he probably wouldn't like the theatre much, either.'

'He hates anything that he thinks is pretentious,' Signora Ricci said.

'You're telling me. You should've heard him about the art I was going to put in Tonielli's,' Carenza said dryly. 'So do you have any idea where I can find something really good to say thank you, something he'd never think of doing for himself because—well, he always puts himself last—but he'd really, really like?'

Signora Ricci gave her an appraising look. 'You know, you're not what I expected.'

Carenza had a pretty good idea what the older woman had thought of her. 'A princess, you mean?'

Signora Ricci looked embarrassed. 'Yes.'

'I could shake him when he calls me that. Except he's been really good to me. He didn't have to help me, but he's been brilliant. And patient.'

Signora Ricci raised an eyebrow and laughed. 'Dante, patient?'

Carenza thought of the way he'd ripped off her knickers, and blushed. 'Sometimes.'

'Well, I'm Mariella.' Signora Ricci extended her hand. 'Nice to meet you, Carenza.'

'You, too, Mariella.' Carenza shook her hand warmly. 'So, can you give me any ideas of the sort of things he likes?'

'Did you know it's his birthday soon?'

'No. He never said a word to me.' And Carenza had a feeling he was going to downplay it. Not because he had issues about his age, but because he never spoiled himself, never took time for fun. A crazy idea formed in her head; the more she tried to suppress it, the more insistent it became. 'Can I ask you something mad—and ask you not to say anything to him?'

'That depends,' Mariella said carefully.

'He's been my mentor, teaching me how to be a serious businesswoman. I want to do a bit of mentoring in reverse, and teach him to have fun.' Taking it much further than she'd planned for tomorrow night.

'First, you'll have to get him to stop working for long enough,' Mariella said dryly.

'This is where my mad idea comes in. Knowing Dante, he'll be working on his birthday. So is there any chance you can move his meetings for that day and the next, and block out the whole time for me instead—but without telling him?'

'And what exactly are you planning to do with him?' Mariella asked.

Carenza told her, and Mariella smiled. 'He'll have a hissy fit on you.'

'No, he won't. You know how he hates people talking about him. When he finds out, he'll be in an airport. Among loads of people. He's not going to make a scene.'

'You're devious.' Mariella gave her an approving look.

'I'll need his passport. I can hardly ask him to bring it with him. Oh, and there's packing.'

'I can sort that out for you,' Mariella said. 'Tell me what you need, and I'll make sure everything's ready in a case under my desk.'

'That's fantastic. Thank you so much.'

'One other thing. He always spends his birthday evening with his family.'

Ah. Carenza hadn't thought of that. 'Then I guess I ought to run this by them first.'

'I can't give you his mother's number. But if I accidentally leave my contacts book open on my computer and go to the toilet, I can't help it if you're incredibly nosey and look on my screen, can I?'

Carenza laughed. 'And you say I'm devious?' She gave the secretary a high five. 'Thank you, Mariella. This is going to be perfect.'

CHAPTER NINE

TEN o'clock on a Saturday night. Before Dante had met Carenza, he would've been working. Maybe in his office, maybe helping out in one of the restaurants, but definitely working. If anyone had told him a few weeks ago he'd be going clubbing with her—and even looking forward to it, just a tiny bit—he would've laughed.

You'll definitely like my dress. And my shoes.

He wondered just what she had in mind. Possibilities bloomed in his head. One thing he did know, he was going to enjoy peeling her dress off afterwards. And so was she.

It still bothered him, the way she'd kissed him goodbye and left on Wednesday. Casual as anything. As if he didn't really matter to her. Which was ridiculous. He didn't *want* a relationship with her. He didn't want to let her close, let her loosen his control over his emotions.

And yet, if he was honest with himself, part of him was starting to wish for exactly that.

'Get a grip,' he told himself sharply as he climbed out of the taxi and rang her doorbell.

The chances were, someone as high-maintenance as Carenza Tonielli would take hours to get ready to go out. Admittedly, she'd never once been late for a mentoring session with him; but this wasn't one of their normal mentoring sessions. He'd agreed to let her set the agenda tonight. And he didn't have a clue where this was going to take them.

She answered almost immediately and Dante's jaw nearly hit the floor. She was wearing the highest heels he'd ever seen, her dress was short and clung in all the right places, and her hair was loose and looked incredibly sexy.

'Let's forget the dancing. I'll tell the taxi driver to go home.' Even to him, his voice sounded rusty, thick with desire.

She just laughed. 'No way. I'm looking forward to going dancing.' Mischief sparkled in her eyes. 'I told you you'd like my dress.'

'I'd like to take it off you, even more.'

A dimple appeared in her cheek. 'Later. You know, patience is a virtue. And a business asset.'

'Oh, yeah?' He had a feeling that they'd both be at fever pitch by the time he took her home. 'Just tell me this club isn't going to be full of sixteen-year-olds.'

She laughed. 'Of course not. We're both too old for that kind of place.'

'So where are we going?'

'Somewhere they play decent music.'

She clearly wasn't going to tell him. Worse still, when he opened the door and ushered her into the taxi, by the time he'd got in she'd already given the driver directions to the club and was chatting to him as if she'd known him her entire life.

Carenza definitely had people skills. He'd take back everything he'd said about her being a spoiled princess who didn't know her staff or care about them. She might have a carefree attitude, but she cared, all right. And she made the world around her sparkle.

The taxi pulled up outside a shabby-looking building. Not promising, Dante thought, but he was careful to keep his voice neutral as he asked, 'When was the last time you came here?'

'About three years ago,' she admitted. 'But I did check with Lucia. My best friend,' she added. 'Lu says it's still the same.'

'So why didn't you go dancing with her?'

'Because she's six and a half months pregnant and she'll have been tucked up in bed for—' she checked her watch '—about the last two hours.'

He held the door open for her, paid for their admission, and his heart sank as he heard the music. It really wasn't to his taste, but he'd promised to take her dancing so he'd just have to put up with it. He was relieved to discover that she'd been right about one thing; most of the people there were over twenty-five, so he didn't feel completely out of place.

'What can I get you to drink?'

'Still water, please.' His surprise must have shown on his face, because she smiled. 'We're dancing. I don't want to get dehydrated.'

'OK.' He ordered their drinks.

When she led him onto the dance floor, he could see admiring glances from the men round them, and the envy on their faces when she made it very clear that she was with him.

This really wasn't something he did. Ever. Even in his teens, Dante had been too busy working and trying to better himself to go clubbing. When he'd bought his first business, most of his time and energy had gone into building up the business a bit more and a bit more still. Sure, he'd dated and gone to the odd party, but he'd kept all his relationships casual and ended them before things got too emotionally involved.

Right at that moment, he felt completely out of his depth.

He wished he'd paid more attention during his teens. He had no idea how you behaved in a club.

Carenza seemed to know. She was smiling, waving her arms about and clearly having a good time. Half the people on the dance floor were doing the same moves that she was; clearly this was a song they all knew and there were set movements to it. He didn't have a clue what they were. And he felt completely out of place here.

'Come on, get with the beat,' she teased. 'I thought all Italian men had a good sense of rhythm?'

'Not this one.' He grimaced. 'Can we go?'

'We've only just got here, Dante.' She stroked his face. 'I know I said we'd leave if you really hated it, but you haven't given it a chance. Just relax. Go with the flow.' She drew him closer. 'Follow my lead.'

Now that was definitely something he wasn't used to doing, following someone else's lead. But he watched what she did, copied the moves. And, to his surprise, he found himself enjoying it. The dancing itself he could take or leave, but he loved seeing the sheer joy and exuberance on her face.

So this was what made her tick. What made her shine.

A nagging little voice in his head pointed out that he wanted to make her shine like this, too. That he knew just how to do it.

He rested his hands on her hips and fitted his movements to hers; her smile grew just that little bit wider, and finally he found himself relaxing.

But then there was a cold feeling at the base of his spine. Automatically he turned round to see what was going on. A man by the bar was shouting at his partner; Dante couldn't hear the words over the volume of the music, but there was an ugly look on the man's face. An ugly look he'd seen too many times on his father's face—just before he raised his hand to strike Dante's mother. Dante's antennae had become so finely tuned throughout those years that he could spot a situation like this right at the earliest stages.

He glanced round, but couldn't see any bouncers anywhere.

Hell, hell, hell. He couldn't just stand by and let this happen.

He leaned forward so his mouth was by Carenza's ear. 'There's a problem—can you go to the door and ask one of the bouncers to come to the bar?'

She looked worried. 'But, Dante—'

'Just go, Caz,' he said, knowing that he sounded abrupt but also knowing that there wasn't time to argue; he needed to stop this happening.

He reached the couple just as the man raised his hand to hit the woman. 'Is there a problem here?'

The other man looked at him, curled his lip and swore. 'Keep your nose out. This is none of your business.'

His voice was slurred; he'd clearly been drinking, and the situation pressed every single one of Dante's buttons. He'd been there too many times in the past, and if he could stop someone else being there, he damned well would. 'Correction. It's my business when a coward starts hitting a woman,' Dante said. 'Leave her alone.'

The man stared at the woman and then at Dante. His expression grew even uglier. 'Are you one of her fancy men?'

'I've never seen your partner before in my life, but that's not the point. Hitting is wrong.'

The man swore again. 'She deserves it.'

'Nobody deserves to be hit. Violence doesn't solve anything.'

'Want to make something of it, then?' The man took a clumsy swing at Dante.

Ha. He'd learned to block blows years and years ago. In

a matter of seconds, Dante had twisted the man's arm behind his back and pinned him against the bar. It would be
oh, so easy to twist that arm a little harder, feel it crack, so
the man couldn't use it to hit her again. It wouldn't be the
first time Dante had done it.

But he felt the anger simmering through him and made
a conscious effort to hold it in check—and to hold the man
immobile rather than hurt. 'That really wasn't your best
idea,' Dante said coolly.

A burly man materialised beside him. 'What's going
on?'

'The guy's drunk, and was about to hit this woman.'
Dante nodded at the woman who was cowering by the
bar. 'I think he might need a little time to cool down a bit.
Police custody, maybe.'

The bouncer nodded. 'I'll deal with it. Thanks for step-
ping in.'

'No problem.' Dante stood to one side to let the bouncer
deal with the drunk. 'Are you OK?' he asked the woman.

She was shaking. 'Thank you,' she whispered. 'But he
can't go to jail.' She shuddered. 'Tomorrow...'

'Look, you don't have to put up with being treated like
that.' He took a business card from his pocket and scribbled
the number of the refuge on the back. 'Ring this number.
Someone will help you. Have you got kids?'

She nodded.

'They'll help the kids, too.'

Her eyes filled with tears. 'He doesn't mean to be like
that. It's just the drink talking. He's always sorry the next
morning.'

'And then you tell everyone you walked into a door?'
Dante asked, remembering his mother's explanations.
'There's no excuse for hitting your partner. He needs pro-
fessional help to get his drinking and his temper under

control. Even if you don't care what happens to you, think of what your kids are seeing. What it's doing to them.' He thought of what it had done to him, years of seeing his father hit his mother and knowing there wasn't a thing he could do about it because he was too young and too small to stop him.

'I… You're right.' She dragged in a breath. 'I'm just so scared of what he'd do if I ever left him.'

'That's what the refuge is for. They'll keep you safe. Ring them,' Dante said.

Carenza watched as Dante scribbled something on the back of what looked like a business card, and ice trickled down her spine. But he'd come here to the club with *her*. He surely wouldn't be chatting up another woman. She had no idea what kind of problem he'd seen, though clearly something had happened because the bouncer she'd spoken to by the door was frogmarching a man out of the club.

Dante turned around and saw her watching him; he left the other woman without a word and came over to her.

'Everything all right?' she asked.

'Yes.' But there was a tightness in his face that worried her. 'Let's get out of here.'

'That guy—did he hit you or something?' she asked.

'No,' he said shortly.

So what was wrong? Why did Dante suddenly look so angry? 'Do you know that woman?'

'No. Can we please just go?' His voice was very, very curt.

She subsided and followed him out of the club.

As soon as they were outside, he made a phone call, then frowned. 'The taxi can't pick us up for thirty minutes. We'll walk.'

She blinked and pointed at her shoes. 'I can't walk home

in these.' She could dance in them for a while, but if they'd stayed at the club for much longer she would've ended up dancing barefoot. And she certainly couldn't walk back to her flat—or Dante's—in them.

He stared at her, then impatience flickered across his face and he scooped her up, clearly intending to carry her.

And he was holding her way too tightly for comfort. 'Ow, Dante, you're hurting me,' she said.

As her words registered he went white and immediately set her on her feet. 'I'm sorry. I…' He shook his head, words clearly failing him, and a muscle worked in his jaw.

Something was obviously very badly wrong.

'I didn't mean to hurt you,' he said in a whisper.

'I know you didn't.' She rubbed her side. 'Dante, what's going on?'

'Nothing.'

It was the biggest, fattest lie she'd ever heard, but he clearly wasn't going to talk. Not here. 'Let's just get away from the club,' she said softly, and took his hand.

He walked beside her, but she had a feeling that he wasn't seeing anything around them. He was lost somewhere else, and she had no idea what was going on in his head.

At the end of the street there was a bar. It wasn't perfect but at least it would be quieter than the club. She dragged him inside, made him sit down with a glass of sparkling water, and rang the taxi firm she normally used to book a cab home. She reached across the table and laced her fingers through his, willing him to talk to her, but he'd gone absolutely silent. She'd never seen him like this before, and it really worried her.

When the taxi took them back to her place, Carenza knew that if she asked him up he'd refuse; he'd go back to his place and brood, and she had no intention of letting him do that. Whether he liked it or not, Dante was going to talk to her. 'See me up to my front door?' she asked.

'Sure.'

Just as she'd hoped, his impeccable manners made him get out of the taxi first. Before she joined him, she shoved a large note at the driver. 'As soon as I get out, drive off, please,' she said quickly.

'What about your change?'

'Keep it.' Money wasn't important. This was.

'Thanks, *bella*.' The taxi driver did exactly as she asked.

'What the…?' Dante began as the cab pulled away.

'My kitchen. Now,' she said firmly. He looked absolutely haunted, and no way was she going to let him go back to his place in this state.

Once he'd sat down at the table, she heated some milk, added a little brown sugar and cinnamon, and then placed the mug in front of him. 'This is better for you than an espresso at this time of night,' she said. 'Drink.'

He made a face, but did so.

'I'm sorry,' he said again. 'I didn't mean to hurt you.'

'I know.' Just as she hadn't intended this evening to be such a nightmare for him. She paused. 'So *did* you know that woman?'

He shook his head. 'I've never seen her before.'

She needed to know the truth. 'I saw you write something on the back of a card and give it to her.'

Dante looked at Carenza. He had a choice: he could either let her think he'd given the woman his number and he was cheating on her—which would hurt her and wasn't true anyway—or he could tell her the truth and would no doubt have to field some awkward questions. But there was no demanding, shrewish look on her face; she clearly feared the worst and was trying to bite back the hurt, just as he'd done so often in his life. Which made the decision easy for him. 'It was the number of a refuge.'

She frowned. 'How do you know the number of a refuge?'

'I...' This was really hard for him to talk about. But he owed her the truth. 'I support it.'

'Support?'

The question made him squirm; he hated people banging on about the work they did for charity. In his view, the people who shouted loudest about it were the ones who cared the least; they were doing it to make themselves look good, not because they wanted to make a real difference. 'Charitable donation,' he muttered.

'Why would you support...?' Carenza began. Then she remembered what her grandfather told her about Dante having a hard time as a child. The fact that there hadn't been a photograph of his father in Dante's flat. And suddenly it all fell together. 'So that's why you don't let people close.'

'What?' He stared at her, looking shocked. 'You're jumping to conclusions. Wrong ones.'

'No, I'm not. Nonno said you had a hard time as a child. He wouldn't tell me any more than that, didn't break any confidences,' she reassured him swiftly. 'But if you support a refuge now, there's a pretty good chance that you do it because a refuge once helped someone you know. And if it happened when you were a kid, my guess is that it was your mum.'

Hearing it spoken out loud made him flinch. She noticed and took his hand. 'I'm sorry. I didn't want to reopen old wounds. I just want to understand what makes you—well, *you*.'

'I wish you really were an airhead princess,' he said. 'Then you wouldn't even have noticed, let alone worked it out.'

'That's why you went to rescue that woman. Because you've seen it happen before.'

'Yes.' He swallowed hard. 'Caz, I really don't want to talk about this. Back off. Please.'

That last word stopped her asking any more. Instead, she pushed her chair back, walked round to his side of the table and wrapped her arms round him. 'I'm so sorry that tonight brought bad stuff back for you. It was meant to be fun. You and me.'

'It's not your fault. You weren't to know this would happen.'

'Do you think she'll be all right?'

He shrugged. 'The first step is the hardest. If she just has the courage to ring that number, then she'll get the help she needs.'

Was that how his family had got the help they needed? she wondered. Not that she was going to ask. This was clearly too painful for him—and he'd asked her to back off. So she just held him, willing him to take strength from her. To let himself lean on her.

And eventually he moved, settled her on his lap and kissed her. 'Thank you. For not judging. For not pushing.'

His words put such a huge lump in her throat, she couldn't answer him. All she could do was kiss him. Softly. Gently.

Except, as always, desire flared between them. The kiss turned hot, and the next thing she knew they were in her bedroom and Dante was peeling her dress off.

He flinched when he saw the bruise on her side. 'Oh, Caz. I'm so sorry. I never meant to hurt you.'

She twisted so she could see the bruise for herself, and sighed. 'I have my mum's very fair English skin—bruises show up quickly. Look, Dante, it was an accident.'

But he still looked utterly horrified. Disgusted with himself.

She stroked his face. 'Dante, I know you'd never hurt me deliberately. It's like… Oh, I dunno, if I was drying up a glass and the stem broke. It's a completely different thing from if I'd thrown it at a wall in a fit of temper.'

'The glass would still be broken,' he pointed out.

'But it's the *intent* that matters. There was some trouble in the club, you sorted it out, and then you wanted to get me out of there as quickly as possible. You were trying to protect me. And this was an accident.' She reached up to kiss him. 'Don't back away from me now. I think we both need this.'

The expression in his eyes was tortured, but he returned her kiss. And when he finally eased into her it was the sweetest love-making she could remember. Ever. There was a tenderness there that had never existed between them before.

And that was the moment she realised she was falling for him. That this was so much more than just hot sex. Just for a moment, he was letting her close—something she re-alised now he found so very hard to do—and this was re-ally, really special.

'Stay tonight?' she asked softly—and regretted the ques-tion immediately, because she could see him closing off again.

'Best not,' he said. But his touch was gentle as he stroked her cheek. 'Stay there. You look comfortable. And cute.'

She could push it, but she didn't want to break this fragile new understanding between them. She wanted to strengthen it. 'OK. Call me later.'

'Yeah.' Intense yearning passed briefly across his face, but he clearly wasn't going to let himself give in, because the brooding businessman was back.

As she heard the front door close behind him her heart bled for whatever he'd seen in his childhood. In her view, having a cruel father was much worse than her own situation, growing up with no parents at all but knowing every day how much she was loved. Yes, there was a big hole in her life, and she missed her parents still, but she'd never known anything but love and kindness from her grandparents. Dante's childhood had clearly been wreathed in shadows. And how she wanted to make things brighter. To fix it.

CHAPTER TEN

THE next morning, Carenza's doorbell buzzed. Dante? she wondered with a surge of pleasure, and pressed the intercom. 'Hello?'

'Signorina Tonielli?' It wasn't a voice she recognised, and she tamped down the disappointment. 'I have a delivery for you.'

She opened the door to discover a huge bouquet of the most gorgeous white flowers—roses, lilies, lisianthus and freesias. On a Sunday, this would have to be a special order. She signed for it with a smile, knowing who they were from before she even opened the card. Familiar spiky handwriting, with the simple message, *I'm sorry. D.*

She buried her nose in them, inhaling the scent. Beautiful. Like the man himself.

She could call him to thank him. Then again, she had a better idea. Especially on a bright, sunny Sunday morning.

Half an hour later, she walked into Dante's office. 'Hi.'

He looked up from his computer. 'Hi.'

'The flowers were lovely. I wanted to come and say thank you properly.' She sat on the edge of his desk, pushed her sunglasses up to the top of her head, and leaned forward to kiss him. 'Though you really didn't need to. You have *nothing* to apologise about.'

He sucked in a breath. 'But I hurt you.'

'Unintentionally.' She stroked his face. 'Though I get why it's a big deal for you.' Seeing the concern thicken in his eyes, she added hastily, 'What we talked about last night, that stays with me. But I know you'd never hurt me. I trust you, Dante. Completely.'

Dante saw the sincerity in her face and his chest felt tight. 'How can you?'

'Because you're a good man. Look at what you've done for me, a complete stranger. You're helping me get my grandfather's business back on track. You do charity stuff without saying a word to anyone about it or expecting anything back. You're something else, Dante Romano.'

This time, when she leaned forward to kiss him, he scooped her onto his lap. He let himself enjoy her warmth, her sweetness. It felt oddly as if she were starting to heal him from the inside out.

'I know you're busy, but I have a teensy proposition for you,' she whispered.

His body surged at that. 'Would that be anything like the first time you propositioned me?'

She flushed deeply at that, and he couldn't help smiling at the outrage on her face when she protested, 'I didn't proposition you.'

'No, Princess? I seem to remember you asking me to mentor you, and offering to pay me in kind.'

She narrowed her eyes at him. 'You misinterpreted me.'

But her eyes were sparkling, and he warmed to his theme. 'And then you took your top off.'

'Because you told me to.'

'And Carenza Tonielli *really* takes orders from other people,' he drawled. 'Not. You did it because you wanted to.'

'And who was it who asked me to go home with him

and do him?' she pointed out, laughing. 'That was a hell of a lot more of a proposition.'

He shifted. 'Mmm. Great idea. Shall I lock the door?'

'No. I mean a different proposition.' She took a deep breath. 'Yesterday didn't go quite as planned. So I'd like to try again.'

His spirits plummeted. 'Dancing?' he asked warily.

'No. So can I borrow you for, say…two hours?' She smiled at him. 'And if I can help you catch up on the time you're losing, just say what you need me to do. I won't mind if you boss me about.'

His heart melted. She wouldn't have a clue about the franchise stuff. Well, he amended, she'd learned a lot, but not enough to be of any real help. But her willingness disarmed him. 'Two hours.'

'Just while it's sunny.'

He was going to have to work *really* late tonight to catch up. He should say no. But his mouth had other ideas. 'I'm all yours, Princess.'

'Good.'

She took him to the Villa Comunale, the main public park in Naples overlooking the sea. And Dante was surprised to discover just how much he enjoyed strolling hand in hand with her in the lush greenery, looking at the fountains and the statues. Something he'd never let himself have the time to do before.

When they came to the roller-skating park, Carenza removed her sunglasses again and looked straight at him. 'Dare you.'

'I've never been skating.'

She grinned. 'Then I'll teach you.'

'If I fall over, I'm going to want to be kissed better,' he warned with an answering grin.

'Deal.' She kissed him lightly, then hired skates for them both.

'You've done this before,' he said as she pirouetted before him on her skates.

She nodded. 'My grandparents used to take me here when I was small. I guess it's like riding a bike or swimming—once you can do it, you don't forget.'

He fell over twice; she didn't laugh, just held her hand out to him to help him to his feet again and smiled encouragement at him. But by the end of their session he was skating with her, as carefree as she was and enjoying every second of it.

Two hours turned into four. Because it would've been rude not to take her out to lunch, afterwards, at one of the little *caffès* overlooking the sea. But when they finally got back to his office, he held her close. 'Thank you.'

'What for?'

'Mentoring me.' He gave her a lopsided smile. 'In having fun. Because I did.'

'My pleasure.'

He could see in her eyes that it wasn't just a pleasantry; she absolutely glowed with the knowledge that she'd given him something special.

'I'd, um, better let you get on,' she said.

'Yeah.' Funny how work didn't seem quite as important as it usually did. Which should worry him. He couldn't afford to lose his focus. 'I'll call you later. And I'll see you on Wednesday for mentoring.' If he could stay away from her for that long.

He managed it. Just. Though there were several texts between them, and a phone conversation that really heated Dante's blood.

But on Wednesday, when he arrived at Carenza's office,

he saw that her eyes were red and her face was blotchy from crying.

It was the one thing he really couldn't bear, seeing a woman cry. Not the fake tears of a woman who wanted to get her own way—he knew that Carenza was more likely to ask outright than to cry pretty little tears designed to make someone change their mind—but real pain and despair. He'd seen too much of it in his life, and it never got any easier. He still couldn't deal with it.

He wrapped his arms round her and held her close. 'What's happened?'

'I'm sorry. I should've cancelled. I can't think straight enough for business, tonight.'

'Doesn't matter. What's wrong, Caz?'

She was shivering. 'My grandparents.'

He remembered what she'd told him about her grandfather's heart problems. 'Gino's ill?'

She shook her head. 'My English grandparents.'

'They're ill?'

'No. They sent me some files.' She was clearly trying to hold back the tears, but a sob escaped. 'They'd been clearing the attic and found some cine films everyone had forgotten about.'

'Of your parents?'

She nodded. 'They were taken when I was two and my parents took me to Cornwall. My grandparents had it transferred to digital media and they emailed it over today.' She stepped back out of his arms and gestured to the computer screen. 'I put a copy on a DVD for Nonno and Nonna. But I watched it first, and it just—it just…' Her words were choked off on a sob. 'How much I've lost.' Her voice was a hoarse whisper. 'I mean, I love Nonna and Nonno. They've done so much for me, and I couldn't have asked for anyone better to bring me up. But it's not the same as having my mum and dad.'

'How old were your parents when they died?' he asked gently.

'Mummy was twenty-six and Papa was twenty-eight—the same age I am now. That's so young to die. And all because of a stupid man who drove too fast on a motorway and…and…and it's all so senseless. So *pointless.*'

She was really, really hurting. And he couldn't walk away. He wrapped his arms round her again and let her cry, holding her tightly until her sobs had died away.

'You've put it on DVD, you said.' He nuzzled her cheek. 'Forget business. Let's go and watch it together.'

'But you hate films.'

'This is different. It's all about you as a child. And I think right now you need to see it with someone, rather than breaking your heart while you watch it all on your own.'

Carenza couldn't believe how thoughtful Dante was being, how tender and how careful of her feelings. For a moment, she wondered if maybe he was actually falling for her, the way she was for him—but no, that was ridiculous. She was just in a state because of all the memories and all the loss coming back to her. Being overemotional, and clutching at straws. He was just being kind, that was all. Being strong. Being Dante.

In silence, she led him up to her flat. Once she'd set the disc in the player, Dante drew her over to the sofa with him and settled her on his lap, wrapping his arms round her. Right at that moment, she really needed the warmth of his body next to hers. And she really appreciated the fact that he could read her mood so well.

'Your mother was beautiful, so like you,' he said softly. 'How old is she there?'

'Twenty-two.'

'She was very young.'

Carenza nodded. 'She met my dad at university in Rome. He was doing business studies and she was doing history of art. They fell in love with each other, and then I came along. I wasn't planned, but that didn't matter because they loved each other and they loved me. My mum didn't finish her degree, but Nonna says nobody minded because they had me—and she stayed in Italy because she wanted to be with my dad.'

'They look really happy together.'

He sounded wistful—or was that just her imagination? Right at that moment, she couldn't trust anything she was feeling.

'They were.' She dragged in a breath. 'When I went to England, my grandparents said it was like seeing my mum's ghost. I mean, Nonna always sent them school photographs and what have you, but it wasn't the same as actually seeing me.' She rubbed away the tears. 'My birthday last year was a nightmare. Turning twenty-seven made me older than my mum was when she died.'

'Tough to deal with,' he said.

'I went off the rails a bit,' she confessed. 'You know about that.'

'Not everything.' He stroked her hair. 'You took drugs?'

She shook her head emphatically. 'Absolutely not. It's never appealed to me—especially after seeing the mess a couple of my friends were in before their family got them into rehab. No, I just partied a lot, danced until three in the morning, drank too much champagne, and went out for smoked salmon and scrambled egg breakfasts. I suppose I wanted to celebrate life, go over the top to prove to myself that I was still here.' She sniffed. 'And I should probably tell you that I slept with way too many men.'

'I already knew that.' Though there was no condemnation in his voice. 'And now I know why.' He shrugged. 'I guess I would've reacted the same way.'

Her chest felt tight. 'That's the other reason I haven't dated for the last year—because I wanted to get my self-respect back.'

'And have you?' His voice was gentle.

'I don't know.'

He kissed her lightly. 'Your parents would be very proud of the woman you've become, Caz.'

The lump in her throat was so huge, she could barely get the words past it. 'You think so?'

'I *know* so,' he said softly. 'I look at what you've done over the last month or so, and I'm proud of you.'

It wasn't just the words; it was his tone. He meant it. It was too much for her, and she ended up bawling all over him again.

By the time she'd stopped crying, his shirt was wet. 'I'm sorry.'

'It's OK. It'll wash. Stay here.' He kissed her swiftly, then moved her off his lap onto the sofa. She curled up in a ball, feeling miserable; when he came back, she realised he'd made her a mug of hot milk and cinnamon. Just like the drink she'd made him, the night he'd trusted her with some of his own shadows.

And that made her cry again. 'You're being so nice to me, Dante.'

'Because you're upset and you need comfort.' He gave her a wry smile. 'I can be nice. Sometimes.'

'When you're not being a brooding business tycoon.' She dragged in a breath. 'Sorry. You didn't sign up for this.' Not as her mentor and not as her lover. And she still couldn't hold the tears back. Surely she should be all cried out by now? But it felt as if there were a bottomless well and she'd never stop crying again.

You're upset and you need comfort.

And he was here for her.

'Dante, I know it's a lot to ask, but will you—will you stay with me tonight? Please?' she whispered.

Stay with her.

Dante knew it would be a bad move. If things carried on like this, he'd get involved with her.

Who was he trying to kid? He already *was* involved with her. Otherwise he would've made some excuse, told her he'd come back when she was feeling better and sort out the business stuff with her. But no. He'd held her close while she'd watched her childhood memories filter across the screen. When the loss had hit her and seared her soul, he'd been there to hold her. Just as she'd held him on Saturday night when his own past had come back to haunt him.

He didn't want to make himself vulnerable to her. But how could he possibly leave her to it? Right now, she was upset and completely defenceless. She really needed him. It just wasn't in him to leave her to it and walk away.

And, although he'd made it a rule never to spend the night with anyone, he'd break it for her. 'Yes. I'll stay.'

He switched off the television and, still holding her close, walked through to her bedroom. Gently, he undressed her. For once it wasn't about needing to rip her clothes off and sate the desire between them, because desire wasn't the uppermost feeling. What that feeling was, he didn't want to examine that too closely—because he had a nasty feeling that he was falling for her. Her brightness, her sweetness, her relaxed and carefree attitude to life.

Bad, bad move. It wouldn't be fair to either of them to make this into a proper relationship. Not when blood ran so deep and he could end up turning into his father. Hadn't he already hurt her, albeit unintentionally? What would happen if he let her dismantle all the barriers and all his control, and they had a fight? Would he end up doing what he feared most—repeating his father's mistakes? Hurting her, the way his father had hurt his mother? And she'd told him that she trusted him completely. How, when he couldn't trust himself?

On the other hand, how could he walk away when she needed him so badly?

Between them, his head and his heart were ripping him apart.

He lay awake for a long time after she'd fallen asleep; the combination of the unfamiliar bed and the unfamiliar warmth against him meant he couldn't just relax. And it felt as if something were cracking inside him.

Much, much later, she moved against him. Murmured his name in her sleep. Pressed her mouth to his skin. And he was lost. When he responded, kissing her back, it wasn't the usual heat between them; this was something different. Something softer, gentler, sweeter. Something that he knew had the power to destroy him.

And, God help him, he found himself welcoming it with open arms.

Carenza had recovered her bounce by their Saturday morning session. She was still wrestling with figures that weren't working out, but she was back to her happy-go-lucky self, teasing him and tempting him. And Dante was shocked to find himself suggesting that they repeat the previous Sunday.

'Challenging me to roller skating?' she teased.

'Or we could go up to Vesuvius, if you want to play with fire,' he teased back.

The look on her face was all the reward he needed.

Maybe, just maybe, this was going to work out.

CHAPTER ELEVEN

ON TUESDAY morning, Dante looked up when he heard the rap on the door at half-past seven, and frowned when he saw Carenza in the doorway. He couldn't remember making an arrangement to meet her today. Particularly at this time of the morning. He was about to ask her what she was doing here, when he realised how rude that sounded, and changed it to, 'I wasn't expecting to see you this morning.'

'I'm your eight o'clock appointment,' she said, surprising him.

Since when? It was the first he'd heard of it.

'And I know it's not eight o'clock yet, but we need to go *now*,' she added, before he could ask.

He looked at her, bemused. 'Go where?'

'You'll see when you get there. Come on, the taxi's waiting.'

'Taxi?' What was she on about? He blew out a breath. 'Princess, I hate to break this to you, but I have a pile of meetings this morning.'

'I know. They're with me. I'm also your nine o'clock appointment. And—' she said with a smile '—just so you know, I'm your appointment for every single slot for the next two days.'

'What?' He wasn't quite following this. Was he having some sort of weird, über-realistic dream? 'How?'

'Mariella moved all your meetings,' she explained.

He felt his eyes widening. 'She did *what*?'

'Don't worry,' she said softly as she rummaged under Mariella's desk and retrieved a small suitcase. 'You're not going to be the hot topic on the staff grapevine or anything. I happen to know what today is, and this is my way of saying thank you for helping me with all the mentoring stuff. Mariella approves. She says you work too hard.'

He blew out a breath. 'If you know what today is, then you also know that I have plans for tonight.'

'Ah. They've also moved by two days. Your mum says you work too hard, too.'

He stared at her. 'You spoke to my mother?'

'We had coffee. And pastries. Um, and we had lunch, the other day.' She retrieved an envelope from the top drawer of Mariella's desk and checked inside. 'Good: your passport. I like your mum, by the way.'

And he'd just bet that his mother liked her, too.

Suddenly, it was hard to breathe. It felt as if someone had just dropped him into the gladiator's den at the amphitheatre in Pompeii and told him he was going to fight a whole pack of lions, single-handed and with no kind of armour whatsoever.

Female lions. Scary ones. His mother, his secretary, and…Carenza. He'd had no idea that they'd been plotting together.

'Relax. You're going to enjoy this. Trust me.' She stroked his face. 'Don't go all closed on me and shut me out, Dante. I want to spoil you a bit. What's so wrong about wanting to make a fuss of someone on their birthday?'

He couldn't even begin to tell her that.

'And you're so difficult to buy for. That's why I wanted to give you—well, you'll see.'

'So where are we going?'

'My favourite city in the world.'

Which told him absolutely nothing. Though there was one thing he did know. 'Princess, you don't have the money to take me away anywhere.'

'Yes, I do.'

He remembered what she'd said about paying him for mentoring her; she'd planned to sell her jewellery. Given the way she'd crumbled over the cine film of her parents, he knew that she'd regret selling whatever it was. 'What did you hock?' he asked.

She lifted her chin. 'That's for me to know and you not to ask.' Then she softened. 'If you really want to know, I sold some of my shoes online.'

Her expensive designer shoes. Her big weakness. And she'd given them up for him.

As if the flood of guilt showed on his face, she said, 'They weren't my absolute favourites, I didn't wear them that much and…' She folded her arms. 'Look, some things are just worth it, OK? I wanted to spoil you, Dante. I wanted to do something *nice* for you.'

And he really, really wasn't used to this. Sure, his mother liked making a fuss of him, but Dante had trained her into keeping everything low-key nowadays. Ditto his sister. In his childhood, most of the time they hadn't had enough money to spoil him—and the one occasion he could remember, when his mother had bought him a brand-new bike, had ended up in tears and mangled spokes. And not because he'd fallen off it. Since then, he'd hated the idea of having a big present and, even though money wasn't anywhere near so tight now for his mother and sister, he insisted on nothing more than a card from them at birthdays and Christmas. Or a token gift. A framed photograph of his niece. Something small. Not a big fuss.

Carenza wasn't playing by the rules. And he had a feeling that, even if she did know his rules, she still wouldn't play by them. She was going to do this her way.

'What was that you were saying about "my way or the highway"?' he asked.

'You're so damn difficult.' She thrust the case at him. 'Grab this and lock up behind you, otherwise we're going to get stuck in traffic and miss our flight.'

The taxi took them to the airport, and when Carenza took her case from the back of the taxi he was surprised to see that it wasn't any bigger than his own.

'I'm a seasoned traveller,' she said, following his look and interpreting it correctly. 'I learned the hard way when I was eighteen that it's much better to travel light.'

He followed her to the check-in desk. 'We're going to *Paris*?'

'Yep.' She smiled at him. 'Happy birthday, Dante.'

'I've never been to Paris before.' The words slipped out, unguarded.

'But you've been abroad?'

He rolled his eyes. 'Of course I have. I'm not *that* much of a country boy.'

'Apart from on business, I mean.'

He didn't have an answer to that. 'Paris,' he mused. 'It might be useful for the second phase of my franchise. Once Dante's is established in all the major Italian cities, I can move on to the rest of Europe. London, Paris, Vienna…'

'Oh, no. You are *not* using this as a business trip, doing a recce on where you can expand your empire. We're not working,' she said firmly. 'This is fun, frivolity and—' she laughed '—probably a bit of excess. Especially when it comes to crêpes. I *love* crêpes.'

Gone was the needy woman who'd clung to him last week. Carenza Tonielli was all princess, completely sure of herself and comfortable in her own skin. And there was a sunniness and a sparkle about her that he just couldn't resist.

'So. No business. Pleasure only. Got it?' she asked.

'Got it.'

'Good.' She kissed him swiftly. 'So tell me, why don't you celebrate your birthday?'

'I do celebrate it,' he protested. 'I have dinner with my family.'

'But you spend the day working. Don't you ever want to do something different, spoil yourself a bit? Even if it's— I dunno—just taking the morning off and walking round the harbour, or window-shopping, or going to a gallery or a museum? Something to feed the soul?'

'No. Though I'm not a miser. I do arrange a meal and drinks for all my staff.'

The Italian way: the birthday boy treated everyone else. But she'd just bet he didn't join them. Not because he thought himself too good to socialise with them, but because he hated socialising. And she couldn't for the life of her understand why. He had social skills and wasn't awkward with people—otherwise he certainly wouldn't be a successful restaurateur. She sighed. 'Right. Consider the next two days as more reverse mentoring. If it kills me, I'm going to teach you to have fun.'

'I'm not sure if that's a threat or a promise.'

She looked at him thoughtfully. 'It's probably both.'

The flight was on time; from the airport in Paris, they took a taxi to the city centre. And Dante was stunned by his first glimpse of the city. It was so different from Naples; instead of the dense network of narrow streets he was used to in the historic quarter of Naples, the boulevards here were incredibly wide. The roads had three or four lanes each way, and the pavements either side were equally wide. Everything seemed to be made from white or cream stone, with tall, narrow windows and wrought-iron balconies. And he fell in love with Paris on sight.

'The city of light,' Carenza said softly, 'so wide and open—this is why I love Paris. And it's even better at night.' She smiled. 'Though I must admit, you can't walk around and hear people singing, like we do in Naples, and I miss that.'

Their hotel was just off the Champs Elysées; as soon as they walked into the reception, Dante knew it was seriously expensive. The reception area was made from marble, the seating was plush leather, and the carpet on the stairs was thick enough to sink into. And he also discovered that Carenza spoke fluent French. Yet another hidden depth to her that he hadn't even guessed existed.

Their room was luxuriously appointed, and he felt another flush of guilt. 'Will you please let me pick up the bill for this?' he asked as she started unpacking.

'No. And anyway, I got a discount. I'm a frequent stayer,' she said with a smile.

'How come?' He unpacked his own clothes—which his secretary had packed incredibly efficiently for him. He had a feeling that it had been under Carenza's direction, too.

'When I lived in London, it was so easy to get the train to Paris. I loved having a long weekend in here. Cafés, art galleries, crêpes…and this hotel is the perfect place to stay, because it's so central. Less than five minutes from the Metro.'

'Can I at least buy you dinner?' He kissed her lightly. 'It's my birthday, so traditionally I'm the one who's supposed to buy dinner.'

'In Italy, it is. But we're in Paris, and I'm half English—and I'm used to doing it differently. In England, everyone spoils the person with the birthday. So I'm treating you.'

'Maybe I'd like to treat you, to say thank you for spoiling me?'

She flapped a hand dismissively. 'We'll discuss that later. It's a gorgeous day out there, and I want to take you exploring, not waste time arguing in here.'

They ended up walking the whole length of the Champs Elysées down to the Tuileries, where the leaves on the trees were starting to turn and glinted all shades of copper and bronze and gold in the sunlight. 'We're only here for two days, so we don't have time to do everything I'd like to do,' she said. 'So I'm taking you to some of my favourite bits.'

Maybe, Dante thought, he'd surprise her with a break here in the spring. Or the middle of winter—Paris and all its gardens would look so pretty, covered in snow.

He discovered that playing tourist with Carenza was fun. She made him pose for a photograph in the gardens of the Louvre with his hand cupped by his shoulder, as if he were holding the Eiffel Tower in his hand, and then they queued up for the museum and wandered through the galleries together. 'As this is the biggest museum in the world, we could spend weeks in here,' she said, 'but we only have a couple of days, so we're just to do the whistle-stop version.' She smiled. 'I can show you some art you might actually like.'

'Pictures that look like what they're supposed to be, you mean?' he teased back.

She laughed. 'Yes. I guarantee you'll like La Joconde.'

It was surreal, walking through the museum and suddenly coming across really famous pieces of artwork that were recognised the whole world over. The Sphinx, the Venus de Milo, and of course the Mona Lisa. And then Carenza took him down to the lower floor and made him stand next to the inverted pyramid; the sunshine poured through the glass and cast rainbows everywhere.

'Oh, yes,' she said with a grin, and showed him the picture she'd taken on her mobile phone: himself, smiling, with his hair rainbow-coloured. 'I might just have to send that to your web designer. It'd look great on the "About Dante's" page on your website.'

'Sure it would,' he said, knowing that she was teasing. Or hoping she was. If that photograph went anywhere near his website, he'd be having strong words with his designer.

From there, she took him on the Metro to the Eiffel Tower. 'Queues,' she said with a sigh. 'We're going to be stuck here for at least half an hour. Right. I know what we need. Go and stand in the queue, and I'll come and find you.'

She reappeared a few minutes later carrying two paper bags and two paper cups of coffee.

'Dare I ask what's in the bags?' he asked.

'The best fast food ever.' She handed one over.

He bit into the crêpe. 'Wow. I wasn't expecting it to be this good.' Light, yet lush; sweet, yet spicy. Like Carenza herself.

'Perfect for a chilly autumn day,' she said. 'And don't worry about the carbs, because you're going to burn all that sugar off. We're walking up to the second stage—that way, you have to work for the view and you appreciate it more.'

Dante had thought himself reasonably fit, but he was glad when they finally reached the second stage and were able to look out over the city. And from there they took the lift to the very top, He stood behind her on the observation platform, looking out over Paris, with his arms wrapped round her middle. 'Thank you,' he said softly, kissing the curve of her neck. 'You've given me a special day.' A day like he'd never had in his life. And, although he usually hated surprises and even more than that he hated not being in charge, to his surprise he was enjoying this hugely. He hadn't expected Carenza's idea of a good time to mesh with his, but every moment in Paris had been magical.

She turned round to face him. 'We haven't finished yet, not by a long way.'

And the promise in her eyes made his heart beat that much faster.

They took the lift back to ground level, and headed back to the hotel to change for dinner.

'Dinner's on me,' Dante said. 'Where do you recommend?'

'Actually, we already have a reservation,' she said. 'It's a tasting menu. And I paid up front, so you can't argue over the bill.'

It turned out that she'd booked a table at one of the best restaurants in Paris, and once Dante had tried the first dish he wasn't surprised to learn that the chef had two Michelin stars. The restaurant itself was incredibly romantic, with plush chairs and damask tablecloths and real orchids decorating the tables. And he'd never seen Carenza look more beautiful, in a little black dress and a pearl choker and her hair in a swish updo. It made his heart skip a beat every time he looked at her.

And then, just before coffee, the waiter brought over a cone made out of tiny Parisian *macarons*, with a sparkler coming out of the top.

'It's not actually part of the menu. I told the maître d' it was your birthday and sweet-talked him into asking the chef to do this especially for you,' Carenza whispered.

Why wasn't he surprised that Carenza would have the nerve to ask a Michelin-starred chef for a special addition to the menu? Or that the chef would be perfectly happy to do it for her?

'This is my idea of a Parisian birthday cake,' she said with a grin. 'Happy birthday, Dante.'

'Thank you.' He reached across the table, took her hand and drew it to his lips. 'This is definitely a first.' He couldn't even remember the last time he'd had a birthday cake.

'I'm glad you like it.' Her eyes were sparkling; she was clearly thrilled that he liked her little surprise.

'I more than like it. You're amazing,' he said softly.

The *macarons*—two smooth, soft, flat-topped almond meringues sandwiched together with buttercream in the same pastel colours as the meringues, with a dash of dark chocolate ganache in the centre—were a little too rich for his taste, but no way was he going to spoil her pleasure in this. He knew the bitter coffee would take the cloying taste away.

She checked her watch when they'd finished the *macarons*. 'Righty, let's go for a stroll.'

'You're OK to walk in those shoes?'

She laughed. 'Just because they're designer, it doesn't mean they're uncomfortable, you know.'

Though he could see in her eyes that she was remembering the night they went dancing. When she'd worn shoes she couldn't walk in.

They strolled hand in hand to the Champs Elysées, the wide avenues flanked with clipped trees and lit by wrought-iron lanterns. Carenza led him under the subway and into the middle of the Arc de Triomphe, with the huge French flag billowing from the centre of the arch and the flame burning steadily on the tomb of the Unknown Soldier.

'You're going to have to work for the view again, I'm afraid,' she said with a grin.

There were literally hundreds of narrow spiral stairs; but at last they were at the top and could look down at the traffic, each lane a blaze of white or red from the car lights. Carenza pointed out the buildings illuminated across the city: the Sacré Coeur in the distance on the hill at Montmartre, and the Eiffel Tower lit up and with a huge beam sweeping across the night from the top of the tower.

'I told you Paris by night was something else,' she said softly.

'You're right. It is.' And sharing this with her felt special. There were plenty of other people on top of the arch, but it still managed to feel intimate, as if they were the only two people there.

'Come and look out over here.' She glanced at her watch again, and shivered.

'It's chilly up here. I don't want you to catch cold.' He noticed that she was only wearing a thin wrap over her dress. Nowhere near enough to keep her warm. 'We'd better go down.'

'No way. We have to stay until the hour.'

'Why?'

'We just do. Stop asking questions, Dante. You'll spoil the surprise.'

Another surprise? Well, he wasn't going to spoil her fun. He shrugged off his jacket and slipped it round her shoulders.

'Dante, you'll get cold,' she protested.

'I'm fine.' He was warm from just being with her.

She glanced at her watch again. 'Any second now…'

Then the Eiffel Tower started to sparkle, lights flashing on and off all over the structure. Dante watched in awe. 'That's stunning,' he said. 'It's like a giant sparkler.' Like the one she'd talked the pastry chef into putting on the cone of *macarons*.

'It's a pity your birthday isn't July the fourteenth, or we'd be seeing fireworks as well.'

He smiled. She made him see those anyway.

They watched until the lights had stopped twinkling,

then headed back to their hotel. In their room, she undressed him slowly; he enjoyed unzipping her dress and taking it off her, seeing the sharp contrast between her soft white skin and her black lacy underwear. And he enjoyed even more taking the pins out of her hair and letting it cascade over her shoulders.

Once they were both naked, Carenza went to the mini bar and retrieved a tiny bottle of champagne.

He frowned. 'What's that for?'

'Not to drink.' She gave him a wicked grin. 'It's your birthday.'

He really wasn't following her. Just what did she have in mind?

'Lie down and close your eyes—and trust me,' she added softly.

Trust.

He didn't let himself trust anyone.

But she'd gone to an awful lot of trouble to make today memorable for him. She'd changed his diary, she'd booked the flight and the hotel and the restaurant, and she'd organised that cake. Refusing her now would be churlish. In silence, he lay down and closed his eyes.

She opened the champagne, and the pop of the cork made him open his eyes again.

She eyed the *bateau lit*. 'Even if I had a silk scarf with me, I couldn't tie you to that.' She gave him a speculative look. 'Though I suppose I *could* blindfold you...'

He gave her a wry smile. 'You don't need any props, Princess.' Carenza alone was all he needed.

Needed?

No. He didn't *need* anyone. Wanted, he corrected himself mentally.

'Then close your eyes, Dante.' She kissed him lightly.

'I promised you pleasure. Oh, and if you could hold onto that headboard, that'd be a help.'

He could resist.

Or he could give in.

When she began to kiss her way down his body, he made the choice, and closed his eyes. He held onto the headboard. As she worked her way down his abdomen it grew more and more difficult to breathe. And when she took him into her mouth, he thought he might just've died and gone to heaven.

'Carenza,' he said hoarsely.

She stopped. 'Don't look until I say you can.'

He knew what she was going to do, now. Roll the condom over him, straddle him, and lower herself onto him. And then she'd let him look and enjoy the view.

And then he felt her hair, silky-soft, brush against him. Her fingers curving round his shaft. And then…

Wha-a-at?

The combination of her hot mouth, cold champagne, and the feel of the tiny bubbles of the mousse bursting against his skin simply blew his mind. He heard himself babbling something, but he didn't have a clue what he was saying. All he could focus on was the incredible sensation. And when his climax hit him, he saw more sparkles in his head than he'd seen on the Eiffel Tower, only minutes before.

When he finally recovered, she was lying next to him, her head pillowed on his shoulder and her arm wrapped round his waist. He was holding her very, very tightly.

'I don't think I'm going to ask who taught you how to do that,' he said.

'Actually, you were my first,' she said. 'I shared a flat with this girl in LA, when I was eighteen. She was completely outrageous. And she told me this was her favourite party trick.'

He blew out a breath. 'Some party trick.'

'Yeah.' She looked smug. 'I love the fact that I had you completely helpless and babbling.'

'You did not.'

She grinned. 'Was that a request for a repeat, Dante?'

He backtracked fast. 'Uh, you blew my mind enough the first time.' He wasn't sure he'd survive a second. At least, not in such close succession.

'So you admit that you babbled?'

'OK, OK, I admit it. You had me babbling.'

'*Helpless* and babbling,' she insisted, completely merciless.

'Helpless and babbling.' He kissed her. 'And I'm going to be planning my revenge. By the time I've finished with you, you're going to be helpless and babbling, too.'

She laughed. 'I do hope that's a promise.'

He kissed her again. 'Absolutely.'

He almost, almost blurted out that he loved her—a near-admission that shocked him to his core.

He'd sworn never to fall in love, never to make the mistakes his mother and sister had made. So how come she'd charmed the barriers around his heart into simply falling down for her? How come the only days in his life that felt as if they had colour in them were the days when he saw her? And since when had hot, mutually enjoyable sex turned into an emotion that scared him witless?

Pushing the thoughts away, he said softly, 'Today's been the best birthday I've ever, ever had.'

Her eyes filled with tears. 'Oh, Dante.'

He stroked her face. 'Don't cry, Caz. I just wanted you to know that today's been special. More than special. And I really appreciate it.'

He really appreciated *her*.

He just didn't have the words to tell her how much.

CHAPTER TWELVE

CARENZA half woke, aware that something was tickling her face; it took her a few moments to work out that it was the hair on Dante's chest. She shifted to get more comfortable, and ended up with her face pressed against his neck. And somehow her mouth was open against his skin and she was kissing his throat.

He murmured her name sleepily, and tipped his head back to let her kiss him. She was half lying across him and he shifted, pulling her so that she was on top of him. And then he was kissing her throat, nuzzling her skin, nipping it gently.

She could feel him hardening beneath her, and rocked against him; right now, she really needed to feel him inside her. It was obviously the same for him because he lifted her slightly, then eased inside her as she lowered herself onto him. He wrapped his arms round her and held her close, still kissing her as he thrust into her.

This felt so incredibly good. She loved the power of his body against hers, loved the way he made her feel, each thrust taking her higher. Pleasure rose through her body; heat began to pool in the soles of her feet, then spiralled up through her, tightening and tightening. And then she was falling over the edge. Dante was right there with her, all the way.

As the aftershocks died away he withdrew, gently rolling her onto her side. His body spooned round hers, one hand settling round the curve of her breast and his mouth resting against her shoulder.

Was it her imagination, or did he just murmur, 'I love you, Caz,' against her skin?

Wishful thinking, she decided. It was the kind of thing Dante would never admit, even if he felt it. He was positively phobic about relationships. Given his childhood experiences, she could understand why. But somehow she needed to find a way to get him to open up to her... She drifted back into sleep, still mulling it over.

The next morning, Dante woke her with a kiss.

Carenza smiled and stroked his face. 'Good morning. Did you sleep well?'

'Yes. You?'

'Mmm.' She stretched languidly. 'But I had the most incredibly realistic dream.'

He raised an eyebrow. 'That sounds interesting. Going to share?'

She smiled. 'You. Me. Sex in the middle of the night.'

His smile faded. 'That's odd. So did I.'

And then a really nasty thought hit her. 'We didn't. Tell me we didn't.'

His dark eyes were filled with wariness. 'What are the chances of us both having exactly the same dream?'

She blew out a breath. 'Dante, if it wasn't a dream, then...' This wasn't going to be good, but she had to bring it up. She needed to be honest with him. 'I don't remember using a condom.'

His face went white. 'If you fall pr—'

She pressed her finger against his lips. No. She didn't want him saying that he'd take responsibility if she ended up becoming pregnant. That wasn't what she wanted from him.

What she wanted from him was what she thought he'd said in the middle of the night.

And, judging from the look on his face right now, it had definitely been her imagination. The sex had been real enough, but love...? No. Dante wouldn't let himself love anyone.

She shook herself. 'Don't say a word. It's fine. The chances are pretty low.'

He raked a hand through his hair. 'Carenza, we had unprotected sex. How can you be so—so unconcerned? So casual about it?'

'Think how many people try for babies for months and months and months without conceiving. We had unprotected sex *once*. What are the chances?'

'And how many people have been caught out by "just the once"?' he countered.

'Nothing's going to happen,' she said firmly. 'And I'm starving. I need a shower before breakfast.' And she tried not to mind when he didn't offer to join her in the shower.

Dante could barely breathe. The prospect of Carenza being pregnant... He could just imagine her, exhausted after labour and yet radiant, with a newborn baby in her arms.

Their newborn baby.

And the longing that surged through him horrified him. How stupid could he get? Given that his sister had made exactly the same mistakes as his mother—believing that her partner would change for her when he couldn't, and that her love would be enough to overcome the violence when it wasn't—it was a fair bet that Dante would make the same mistakes as his father. For Carenza's sake, he couldn't risk his past repeating itself. Couldn't risk hurting their child through impatience.

When it was his turn to shower, he turned the water down to cold, in the hope that it would shock some common sense back into him. His life was fine as it was. Just himself and the business. He didn't need anything else.

And he'd make damn sure he never spent another night with Carenza. Because now he knew just how dangerous it could be for his peace of mind.

'So what are the plans for today?' he asked over breakfast.

'Our flight back to Naples isn't until early this evening, so we can spend the day in the city. The hotel's agreed to keep our luggage in storage until we're ready to pick it up—and our taxi's booked to take us to the airport. So I thought I'd show you the other side of the city.'

'That'd be great.' And as long as they talked about Paris or business, and nothing in the slightest bit emotional, everything would be absolutely fine, Dante thought.

It didn't take long to pack after breakfast; and then they took the Metro through to Montmartre. He looked up the incline of the street to the Sacré Coeur, the white domes of the church and the green hill on which it stood standing out against the blue, blue sky. 'That's beautiful,' he said.

She looked pleased. 'Wait until you get to the top. The view of the city from the steps is stunning.'

He discovered that she was absolutely right. And, just round the corner from the Basilica, the streets were narrow and bustling, just as they were in Naples, filled with souvenir shops and delis and cafés—a sharp contrast to the wide boulevards around the Champs Elysées, but this part of Paris felt more like home to him.

She dragged him over to a *gelati* shop.

'Princess, this is an Italian artisan ice cream shop,' he pointed out.

She smiled. 'I know, and Italian ice cream is the best.' When they came out, he was amused when she rattled off a quick assessment, saying where it was better than Tonielli's and where it could learn from her. 'Having said that, this crème brûlée *gelato* is pretty good.' She looked enquiringly at him. 'How's the blueberry and white chocolate?'

He held out his cone so she could taste it.

'Not bad,' she said. 'But I think it'd be better still if you had the blueberry and the white chocolate flavours separate, then rippled them together.'

They strolled through the streets to the historic Place du Tertre, full of cafés and artists selling their work from stalls; Dante could hardly believe how much they'd managed to cram into the centre of the square. People around the edges were performing street theatre and juggling; tourists were sitting quietly while artists drew caricatures and portraits of them.

'Your picture, sir, madam?' an artist asked. 'I can do a special price for the two of you.'

Carenza's eyes lit up and she turned to Dante. 'Can we?'

Had he been on his own, he would've made a polite excuse and walked on; but he could see how much Carenza wanted to do it. The whole Parisian experience. And, since she'd given him so much over the last two days, who was he to deny her something so small? 'Sure we can,' he said.

They sat down on a nearby wall. 'Your arm round the lady,' the artist directed. 'Smile at each other.'

Dante felt awkward and exposed—particularly when other tourists came to look over the artist's shoulder at the picture he hadn't yet seen—but everyone seemed to smile and nod approval at what the artist was capturing on paper.

It was only a few short minutes before the artist showed them the portrait, pastels on rose-grey paper.

And it scared Dante witless.

The way he was looking at Carenza, it was obvious to the whole world that he was in love with her. Oh, hell. Hopefully she'd just think that the artist had taken a bit of—well, artistic licence.

He paid the artist, then on the artist's recommendation went into one of the souvenir shops and bought a tube so they could roll up the picture and keep it protected on the way back to Naples.

Carenza stood on tiptoe and brushed her mouth against his. 'Thank you.'

'Prego,' he said automatically. But he couldn't get the portrait out of his head. Did he really look at her like that? And, if so, had she noticed? Because it really wasn't fair to raise her expectations—to make her hope that he could be something he knew he just couldn't be.

They stopped in a café for a *croque monsieur* and a coffee, and then Carenza took him to the Pompidou Centre.

'It's really impressive, isn't it?' she asked.

He looked at the huge steel-and-glass structure. 'Yes.' Though he didn't like it anywhere near as much as he'd liked the Louvre or the Eiffel Tower. And it didn't even begin to compare to the beautiful white stone buildings across the other side of the city, the ones he'd fallen in love with on sight.

'This is one of my favourite places in Paris.'

The second they walked in, he realised why. It was filled with modern art. And he just didn't get it. The more he walked round, the more he saw, the less he understood. Half the stuff looked as if it had been drawn by a child in kindergarten, and the other half were just random splodges of colour. What was so special about all this? Why did she love it so much? Was it an 'emperor's new clothes' kind of thing, or was he just missing the gene that made him appreciate it?

'If you didn't have Tonielli's, what would you do?' he asked.

She looked surprised by the question; then she smiled. 'That's an easy one. I'd like my own art gallery.'

Just as he'd guessed. 'And you'd sell this kind of stuff?' He looked at the painting of squares in front of him, and others that just seemed a chaotic mess of colour.

'Yes. It's the vibrancy and the energy of the pieces that I like.'

Vibrancy and energy. She could've been describing herself. But he couldn't see it in the works of art. 'I don't get it,' he admitted. 'To me, you could hang this stuff any which way and it still wouldn't make any sense. It's all random.'

She shrugged. 'That's probably what the artist wants you to feel. That the world's mixed up and random.'

He wasn't convinced.

'Art's a personal thing. It's better to go for the stuff that you like—the stuff that makes you *feel* something.' She gave him a rueful smile. 'I guess I was hoping that seeing it all together here would make you see what I see in it.' She sighed. 'I really should've taken you to the Musée D'Orsay instead of here. I think you would've liked the Impressionists more. And Van Gogh.'

'Probably,' he said. 'Sorry. I'm a philistine. I like art to look like what it's meant to be.'

She nodded. 'And this doesn't. OK. Let's go.'

'If you want to stay, I don't mind,' he fibbed.

'Yes, you do—and there's no point in staying if you're not enjoying it. I want you to love Paris as much as I do. And there's somewhere else near here I want to show you— somewhere I think you'll like.'

She led him through the Marais district to the Place des Vosges. 'This is the oldest square in Paris.'

It was a beautifully laid out square with gorgeous buildings, and he liked this a lot more than the modern building she'd just taken him to.

They wandered through the arcaded walkways together; he noticed that there were an awful lot of art galleries among the shops. Carenza was clearly enjoying window-shopping; and then she went very still and gave a sharp intake of breath.

'What have you spotted?' he asked.

'That's gorgeous.' She pointed out a tall, narrow canvas with five wide bands of jewel-bright colours across it. 'But unfortunately the price tag would blow my fritter budget for years.'

'Fritter budget?' It wasn't a term he was familiar with.

'Spending money, for little pleasures. Though some people would see it as frittering my money away. So I might buy myself flowers, or some music, or some luxury chocolate.' She smiled. 'Or I'd save it all up for ages and ages and blow the lot on a piece like that one.'

'It looks almost like a slice of a rainbow,' he mused, 'except there aren't quite enough colours.'

'The blue and purple bands are sky—a midnight sky, I'd say—the green band in the middle's the sea, and the orange and red bands are the beach,' she explained. 'Look at the way they blend into each other. It's gorgeous.'

To him, it was simply five bands of colour; but he liked the effect it had on her, the way it had made her face glow. Now she'd explained it to him, he could see what she meant. Though it still wasn't something he'd choose to hang on his wall.

'Come on, let's go and get a coffee,' she said.

They stopped at a café where they could watch the fountain splashing in the centre and children playing on the grass in the autumn sunshine. 'Did you know that loads of cavaliers duelled here?' she asked.

'I can imagine it,' he said. 'Is this where you'd settle if you lived in Paris?'

'I'd love to,' she admitted. Then she grinned. 'Just think, we could take over a whole corner of the square between us. A branch of Dante's, a branch of Tonielli's, and an art gallery sandwiched between them.' She laughed. 'But there's a slight problem. We'd have to sell everything we owned between us, and we still wouldn't be able to afford three shops here, let alone a flat.'

'A branch of Dante's.' He gave her a thoughtful look.

'No, no, I was kidding—' she held both hands up in a gesture of surrender '—and this *isn't* a business trip.' She finished her coffee and wrinkled her nose. 'Sorry, I need the ladies'. I won't be a minute.'

'No problem.'

Did he have enough time to go back to the gallery where she'd fallen in love with that painting? he wondered. Even assuming that there were the usual queues for the ladies' toilets, he probably didn't. But there was another way to get what he wanted. He whipped out his mobile phone, flicked into the Internet, found the gallery's website, and rang them. It didn't take long to close the deal. The painting would be wrapped securely and sent by international express delivery to Naples, and it would be there at his office on Friday morning.

Perfect.

He was just putting his phone away when Carenza walked back over to him.

'I saw that. You were making a business call, weren't you?' she accused.

He had no intention of telling her what he'd really been

doing. The whole point was for it to be a surprise. And it was sort of a business call. 'Busted,' he said lightly.

'You're impossible.' She glanced at her watch. 'I guess we'd better be heading back. It'll take us a good half an hour to get from here to the Champs Elysées, and the taxi's booked to take us to the airport in an hour.'

To Carenza's relief, everything ran smoothly on the way back. They collected their luggage from the hotel, and the taxi got them back to the airport in more than enough time to check in.

Dante held her close. 'Thank you. These past couple of days have been really special.'

He held her hand all the way back to Naples, and she found herself hoping that those whispered words hadn't been her imagination or wishful thinking. A man like Dante, so used to keeping himself aloof from people, would find it hard to say those words. So he'd say them when he thought she was asleep, wouldn't he?

Maybe she was hoping for too much, but the way his fingers were laced through hers gave her confidence. He cared. He just wasn't used to saying it. With her help, he'd learn.

From the airport, they took a taxi back to her flat. Dante insisted on seeing her to the door.

'Stay here tonight?' she asked.

Though she could see in his face that he was remembering last night, how they'd made love in the middle of the night. Riskily. Without a condom. For a man so in control as Dante, that was a nightmare. And she knew even before he spoke what his answer would be.

'Best not,' he said gently, 'but thank you. You made it the most memorable birthday of my life.'

And I could make every day like that for you, if you'd

let me. Not that she said the words. She knew they'd make
him back away from her even faster.

He kissed her lightly. 'I'd better go. The taxi's waiting
for me. Goodnight, Princess.'

And that was it.

He was gone.

CHAPTER THIRTEEN

On Thursday evening Dante arrived at his mother's house with flowers and chocolates.

'Dante, *amore*.' Gianna hugged him warmly when she opened the door to him. 'And you didn't need to bring me anything.'

'I know, Mamma, but I wanted to.' He hugged her back.

'So did you have a good time in Paris?' Gianna asked.

'Wonderful.' Though it had left him yearning. Wishing for something he couldn't have. Wishing things were different. Not that he'd tell her that. She didn't need the extra guilt.

'Happy belated birthday, little brother,' his sister said, pinching his cheek.

'Less of the "little", Rachele. I've been bigger than you since I was twelve,' he said with a grin.

'I know, but you're still the baby.'

And, talking of babies... 'Is Fiorella still up?' he asked hopefully.

'Oh, yes. No going to bed until she's seen Zio Dante,' Rachele told him, smiling. 'Especially as there's cake involved.'

But as soon as he walked into the living room he could see that his niece was already being entertained. She was having a story read to her—one of her favourites, he recognised, and the little girl was joining in with the refrain. Though the person reading the story was the last person he'd expected to see: Carenza.

'Hi,' she said, giving him a shy smile.

Fiorella looked up. 'Zio Dante!' She wriggled off Carenza's lap and ran to him; he caught her up and swung her round.

'Hello, *bellezza*,' he said with a smile. 'Missed me?'

'Yes,' she lisped. 'Renza read story.'

'I'd better let her finish, then, while I help Mamma and Nonna.'

To his surprise, Fiorella ran over to Carenza again and climbed back onto her lap. Carenza was a stranger, and Fiorella was usually wary of strangers; and yet the little girl seemed to have accepted Carenza immediately. So did this mean Carenza had spent time with his sister and his niece? Or was it that Fiorella responded to Carenza's natural warmth?

He'd never seen Carenza with children before. From what she'd said, Lucia was the first of her friends to have a baby on the way; and Carenza was an only child. As far as he knew, she'd had practically nothing to do with kids. Yet she was patiently telling the story, getting Fiorella to join in with the refrains, and using different voices for each character.

How could he not be charmed?

Then he remembered the other night. In Paris. When they'd had unprotected sex. Despite her protests that everything was fine and her insistence that she couldn't be pregnant, he knew that it was still a possibility. Again, he had that weird kind of flash-forward. He could imagine her holding their baby. Or holding their toddler and reading a story, just as she was doing right now with Fiorella.

He shook himself. Now he was being absolutely ridiculous, and it annoyed him that he reacted to Carenza in this way. He'd never felt like this before about anyone. And it really, really bothered him.

'Mamma, let me help,' he said, fleeing to the safety of the kitchen.

She shooed him out. 'No. Go and sit with Carenza.'

Was she matchmaking? Dante thought suspiciously. And since when had Carenza been invited to his birthday dinner anyway? His mother hadn't mentioned it. And neither had Carenza.

There was no way he could ask without making a fuss. So he gave in and went back into the living room.

'Zio Dante!' Fiorella pointed to the space on the sofa next to them, and smiled. 'Read story, too.'

What could he do? And then he found himself drawn into the story, reading it with Carenza and taking over the voices of some of the characters. Fiorella's eyes were shining with joy, and Dante's chest felt tight.

This was how it could be. Himself, Carenza and their own child. If he were a different person.

If only.

His mother had made her usual fabulous dinner. Carenza joined in with everyone else in helping to clear the dishes between courses. Gianna must *really* like her, he thought, to allow the younger woman in her kitchen. And Carenza fitted right in. As if she were already part of the family. Which scared him even more.

Then his mother came in with a birthday cake, the candles lit. Everyone sang *'Buon Compleanno'* to him, even little Fiorella. He smiled, and blew out the candles.

'You have to make a wish,' Carenza said.

Yeah. And he knew what he would wish for.

But he saw their faces round the table, all full of hope—and he remembered all the times his mother had a black eye or a tooth knocked out or a broken arm. All given to her by the man who was supposed to love her. The man who'd made those vows in front of their joined families. *Nella gioia e nel dolore, nella salute e nella malattia.* In joy and in sorrow, in health and in sickness. Except his father had been the one to cause the sorrow and the sickness.

E di amarti e onorarti tutti i giorni della mia vita. And to love you and honour you, all the days of my life. His father had broken that vow, too.

And the wish turned to ashes in Dante's head.

He'd inherited his father's genes. So it followed that, even if he started with all the good intentions in the world, he could end up hurting Carenza, the same way his father had hurt his mother. And he really couldn't take that risk. For both their sakes.

'You've gone very quiet,' Gianna said.

'I'm fine,' he fibbed.

'You work too hard.' She shook her head in exasperation. 'And, knowing you, you're trying to catch up with the work you didn't do when you were in Paris. Even though Carenza says Mariella moved all your meetings so you're not actually behind at all.'

'I'm fine, Mamma,' he repeated, and forced himself to smile. 'It's Fiorella's bedtime. Let me do the washing up, and then I'll leave you in peace.'

'No, it's your birthday and you're not washing up today.'

'Will you let me wash up?' Carenza asked.

'No, *tesoro*,' Gianna said with a smile. 'Thank you, but it's fine.' She gave Dante a pointed look, and he knew that if he didn't offer to give Carenza a lift, his mother would nag him about it for weeks.

'Can I give you a lift home, Carenza?' Dante asked politely.

'On the bike?' she asked.

He couldn't help smiling, then. 'My mother banned me from riding the bike here.'

'Because it's *dangerous*,' Gianna interjected.

Dante rolled his eyes. 'It's as safe as a car.'

'Not the way you drive, it isn't.'

He shrugged. 'I hate waiting in queues. It's more efficient than a car. But tonight, to keep my mother happy, I'm using a taxi. And your flat's on my way home, Carenza, so if you'd like a lift?'

'Thank you.'

He rang the taxi firm he normally used, and Carenza read Fiorella another story until the taxi arrived. His mother insisted on giving them both neatly wrapped parcels of cake; after hugging everyone goodbye, Dante and Carenza climbed into the back of the taxi.

She reached out to take his hand. 'You're really tense. What's wrong?'

Everything. 'Nothing,' he said through gritted teeth.

To his relief, she didn't push it.

When the taxi pulled up outside her flat, she smiled at him. 'It's not that late. Would you like to come up for coffee?'

'That's not a good idea, Princess.'

'Are you angry with me for gatecrashing your birthday dinner?'

'No.' He was angry with himself. 'Anyway, you didn't gatecrash. My mother invited you.' He blew out a breath. 'Just leave it, Caz. Please. I'll see you later.'

'OK. *Ciao.*'

He made the taxi wait until she was safely inside, then headed for home. His head was pounding and that tightness was back in his chest. Well, tough. Nobody said that life was fair or that you could get what you wanted. And what he wanted had to stay off limits. For Carenza's sake as well as his own.

On Friday morning, as promised, the painting arrived from the Parisian gallery.

Dante decided to give it to Carenza the next evening, when they met for their usual mentoring session. But the parcel disturbed him all day, looming in the corner of his office. Tempting. Giving him an excuse to see her.

In the middle of the afternoon, he gave in and called her. 'Are you busy, this evening?'

'I'm playing with ice cream recipes—but I could do with a taste-tester, if you want to come over.'

'I'd like that. What time?'

'Eight?' she suggested.

'I'll bring pizza with me—Mario's *marinara* is the best in Naples.'

'That'd be good. I'll see you tonight, then.'

Carenza wondered just why Dante wanted to see her tonight. She couldn't help the flutter of excitement down her spine; they'd grown much closer in Paris, so did he want to see her for herself and not the business?

Then again, given how he'd reacted that morning to the possibility of her being pregnant, and the way he'd reacted last night at his family birthday meal, probably not. She still didn't quite understand why he was backing away from her, why he was so insistent that a relationship between them wouldn't work. Over the last few weeks, since she'd got to know him, she'd revised her own opinion on that score. Yes, they came from different worlds; but she thought that they balanced each other nicely. He'd taught her a lot about business, and he'd given her the confidence to run Tonielli's because she was beginning to understand what she was doing. She'd discovered that she had a serious side, and people were at last taking her seriously, thanks to him. And she was teaching him to relax and that you didn't have to work every second of the day, putting some balance back into his life, too. She liked his family, and she was pretty sure that he liked hers, otherwise he wouldn't be mentoring her.

Together, they could be such a great team.

How could she persuade him to give them that chance?

That evening, she almost dressed up and put on full make-up. Then again, that was just surface and Dante saw deeper than that. He would tease her for being princessy if she wore a dress. And she didn't want him to think she was just a clothes horse. She wanted him to take her seriously—as herself, not just in business. So she contented herself with changing into a clean pair of jeans and one of the little strappy tops she knew he liked, left her hair down and brushed it until it shone, and added a slick of lipstick and a touch of mascara.

When he arrived, he was carrying two parcels. 'What's that?' she asked.

'Pizza.'

She rolled her eyes at him. 'I know that—you said you were bringing it. I meant the other box. The one that isn't pizza-sized.'

'All in good time, Princess.'

The teasing smile in his eyes warmed her.

'We'd better eat. The pizza's getting cold.'

It was as good as he'd promised. And there was an expression on his face she hadn't seen before when he looked at her. She couldn't even begin to guess what it meant; but she tried really hard not to hope for too much. To hope that two nights of sleeping away from her had made him realise that he missed her. That his bed, like hers, felt just too big for one.

'New flavours of ice cream, hmm?'

'This one's meant to be hot.' She brought out the first tub from the freezer.

'Hot ice cream?' He gave her a half-smile, and took a spoonful.

'What do you think?'

'Honest opinion?' At her nod, he grimaced. 'Either you overdid the chilli, or it works much better in chocolate bars than it does in ice cream.'

She tried a spoonful. 'Much as I hate to admit it, you're right.'

The blackberry sorbet was much better, and this time she actually got a compliment from him. Then he smiled at her. 'I was going to buy you flowers to say thank you for spoiling me in Paris.'

'You really don't have to.' And clearly he hadn't, because that box wasn't the right size to contain flowers.

'But I thought you might like this a bit more.' He handed her the parcel. 'It's an unbirthday present. Just to tell you that I...' He stopped.

Her heart skipped a beat. And another. Was he going to say it? The words she was so sure she'd heard that night in Paris?

'...I appreciate you,' he finished, looking wary.

Was that Dante-speak for *I love you*?

Or was she hoping for way too much?

She undid the wrappings. It felt like a frame of some kind. And it had been very well wrapped. Wrappings she recognised as the kind she'd used at Amy's gallery.

And then she unwrapped the final bit and saw what he'd bought her.

The painting she'd fallen in love with in Paris.

'Oh, my God. Dante. It's...' Her eyes filled with tears.

'That *was* the one you liked?' he asked, sounding suddenly unsure.

'Yes, but it was hideously expensive.'

He shrugged. 'Money's not important.'

'It's beautiful. And you hate it. Yet you bought it for me.'

'Because it made your face light up,' he said simply.

She felt her bottom lip wobble. 'I think I'm going to cry.'

'No, you're not.'

He looked panicky; obviously he found tears unsettling, and yet he'd let her cry all over him in the past. Especially that time when her English grandparents had sent her the film from her childhood. 'These are happy tears,' she said softly. 'I can't believe you bought this for me and got it sent from Paris.'

'That was the phone call you nearly caught me making,' he said.

She bit her lip. 'And I nagged you because I thought you were working. I'm sorry.'

He shrugged. 'No problem. Now you know what I was doing.'

'It's beautiful.' She looked at it again, then laid it carefully on the table and walked round to his chair so she could kiss him. 'Thank you so much.'

'Prego.'

And now she'd made him uncomfortable again, making a fuss. She'd noticed that in his family's home, too—if his mother or his sister made a fuss of him, he wriggled away. But Fiorella...he was putty in his tiny niece's hands. And she'd just bet that he would read stories to Fiorella, sing songs to her, and sit on the floor and play as many games with the little girl as she wanted.

Which gave her hope that maybe she, too, could reach him. There was definitely a chink in his armour; she just had to find the right way to reach it. 'Dante. Stay tonight,' she said softly.

He shook his head. 'I can't.'

'Can't or won't?'

'Both.'

'Why?'

He stroked her face. 'It's not you: it's me.'

She went cold. Suddenly, everything had changed. Was the painting his idea of a Dear Jane letter, rather than his way of saying 'I love you'? And she'd heard that phrase before, from several Mr Wrongs. *It's not you: it's me.* Just before they'd dumped her.

And when Dante distanced himself slightly over the next few days, missing two mentor sessions because he was up to his eyes in work—that was when she knew he was planning to end it between them.

The week got worse, because then her period started: she felt the familiar dragging sensation, low in her belly, and knew exactly what it meant. She should've been relieved that she'd been right and that night of sleepy, unprotected sex in Paris hadn't left her pregnant.

Except she wasn't relieved.

Because she realised then exactly what was missing from her life. What she wanted. Why she'd really come back home to Italy.

She wanted a family.

Specifically, she wanted to make a family with Dante. To have his children. To have everything that had been taken from her as a child.

But would Dante take a chance on her? Given the way he seemed to be avoiding her, she doubted it.

She brooded about it all day, her mood growing darker and darker. And then she pulled herself together. She was a

Tonielli. She didn't wait to see what life dealt her; she went after what she wanted. And she wanted Dante. She sent him a text. Can I see you tonight? Need a quick chat. She deliberately didn't tell him the subject, knowing that he'd assume it would be about the business. Which was possibly a little devious, but if she told him why she really wanted to talk to him, she knew he'd run a mile.

It was two hours before she got a reply. I'm working late. Tomorrow?

It looked as if she'd have to learn to be patient. Tomorrow's fine. Half-past seven, here?

OK.

The next day dragged. And then finally it was half-past seven, and Dante rapped on the door of her office.

'Hi. Coffee?'

'No, I'm fine. So what's up? Problem with the figures?'

'No.' She indicated the chair opposite hers, and he sat down. 'I thought you'd like to know, my period started yesterday.'

His expression was absolutely unreadable, and his voice gave nothing away when he said, 'That's probably for the best.'

No, it wasn't. Not in her book. Though she couldn't tell him that just yet. She had to work up to it.

'I've been thinking,' she said. 'This thing between you and me, it isn't what it started out being.'

He frowned. 'How do you mean?'

'It's not just about hot sex and mentoring. Not any more.' She took a deep breath. 'You're a workaholic, you're difficult and half the time I don't have a clue what's going on in your head. But since I've got to know you, I've realised...' Once she'd said it, there was no going back from here. But she knew Dante wouldn't say it first. She had to be brave.

Take the risk that he'd reject her. And hope to hell that he wouldn't. 'I love you.'

Emotion flickered across his face, too fast for her to read it: and then he was back to being inscrutable again.

'I'm sorry,' he said. 'I don't feel the same way.'

But there was a tiny flicker in his eyes as he said it. She knew that he was lying—what she didn't understand was *why*. 'That's not true,' she said softly. 'I knew in Paris. It was different between us, that night. And I heard what you said.'

He looked panicky. 'I got carried away.'

'More like you thought I was too sleepy to remember.'

He dragged in a breath. 'OK. I said it. But this can't work—I can't take the risk.'

'What risk?' She frowned. 'I don't understand.'

'I guess I owe you the rest of what I started telling you.' He closed his eyes for a moment. 'This is hard for me. I don't spill my guts. Ever.'

She took his hand. 'It's not weak to talk.'

'Isn't it?'

She sighed. 'I don't want to argue with you, Dante. I just want to understand what's going on in your head, and I can't read your mind. Talk to me. Please.'

'Just promise me—no pity. Ever.'

Why would she pity him? 'I promise. Just talk.'

His words were hesitant at first; then it was as if something had cracked and everything came pouring out.

'I don't remember it being bad when I was tiny, but when I was six or seven my father lost his job and started drinking. When he came home, he'd hit anyone who got in his way or answered him back. He broke my sister's arm, he broke my mother's ribs, he gave my mother black eyes.'

'And he hurt you?' she asked softly.

Dante nodded and swallowed hard. 'The more he drank,

the worse he got; and the less reliable he was when he did get a job. And then he'd lose his job and start drinking and it was a vicious circle.'

Now she understood why he never drank. And no wonder there was no picture of his father on his mantelpiece. She reached over the desk and took his hand.

He pulled away. 'No pity.'

'It isn't pity. It's sympathy. Which is completely different.'

A muscle flickered in his jaw. 'What I hated most was that all the neighbours knew. They *knew*. They talked about it, but they did nothing. They didn't call the police; they didn't tell any kind of authority; they didn't take him to one side and tell him to stop.'

'Maybe they thought he'd take it out on your mum even more if they interfered,' she suggested quietly.

'But they did nothing. They didn't offer her a safe place or try to help her. They just *talked* about her.'

He'd told her a little, that night they'd gone dancing, but she'd had no idea just how bad it had been. And the one thing that shocked her was how he really believed the worst of himself—that he was like his father. But she'd seen no evidence. 'You're not your father, Dante.'

'No, but I have his blood. I have a violent streak.'

'No way.' Dante was incredibly controlled. 'The only time I've ever seen you lose control…' She felt her face heat. He'd been babbling her name. Completely vulnerable. 'No. You're not violent.'

'I keep myself in check. Most of the time,' he added wryly. 'When I was thirteen, I saw my father hitting Rachele. By then, I was almost as big as him. Big enough to do something to stop him. I broke his arm.'

And he thought that made him a thug? 'Dante, you didn't do it because you were enjoying hurting him. You were trying to protect someone who was vulnerable and stop him hurting her. You did the only thing possible. Words wouldn't have stopped him, would they?'

'That's not the point. I reacted on gut instinct—I did things the same way *he* did things. Violence. I can't forgive myself for that.' He dragged in a breath. 'And there's worse. He fell under a tram, the following year, one night when he was drunk. And when I heard the news, I wasn't upset that he'd died. I was glad. Really glad.' He closed his eyes for a moment. 'Worse still, I wished I'd been there to push him under the tram.'

'I think anyone would, in your shoes.'

He shook his head. 'Only someone with my father's bad blood. And that wasn't the only time I hurt someone. Rachele...she made the same mistake as my mother. She thought Niccolo—Fiorella's father—loved her. That her love would change him, make him into someone decent.'

Carenza gave a sharp intake of breath. 'Are you saying that he hit her?'

He nodded. 'When she was pregnant.'

'Oh, Dante.'

'And when I found out, I went round to see him. I pinned him against the wall. I could see the fear in his eyes, smell the sweat pouring off him. My hand was against his throat. I could've crushed his windpipe.'

'But you didn't.' She didn't need to ask. She was absolutely sure that Dante wouldn't do that.

'I managed to keep control. Just. But it was so thin, like gossamer—one wrong word from him, and I would've snapped. I would've killed him.'

'No, you wouldn't, because that's not who you are. And he'd hurt Rachele. You're her brother. Of course you weren't going to ignore what he did and let him get away with it.'

'But violence isn't the way to fix a problem. I was wrong,

Caz. I told him if he laid another finger on her, I'd break every bone in his body—twice. And I meant every single word.' A muscle clenched in his jaw. 'I twisted his wrist hard enough to almost break it. To make sure he knew I meant it.'

'You were protecting your sister, Dante.'

'With the wrong sort of protection. I should've called the police, supported Rachele while she made a statement, made sure that he…' He shook his head. 'I dunno. Got psychiatric help, to sort him out and make sure he didn't do that to anyone ever again. But I didn't. I did things my father's way, with fear and threats and I actually hurt him.' He blew out a breath. 'And that's why I…why this has to end. I can't trust myself. And I don't want to hurt you.'

'You're hurting me by ending this,' she pointed out.

'That's nothing compared to what I might do to you. Supposing the restaurant chain fails? Supposing I end up like my father, taking out my frustrations on you—or, if we have babies, on our children? I can't take that risk. I just *can't*. Don't ask me to try.'

'The restaurant won't fail. You'd never let it. And even if the worst happened, something you couldn't fix—I know you'd never take out your frustrations on me and hurt me. And don't start on about that bruise, either. That was completely accidental and it could've happened to anyone.'

His eyes were filled with pain. 'That's what my mother thought when she married my father. That's what Rachele thought when she started seeing Niccolo. That the men they loved would never hurt them. And they were both wrong.'

'But you're not your father, Dante. You're *not*.'

'I'm his son. I have his blood. Bad blood, maybe. So I just can't take that risk,' he said again. 'We have to end this thing between us. Keep things strictly business from now on. I'm sorry.'

And he walked out of Carenza's flat while she stood there, unable to move or think or act.

Dante was so wrong about this, it was untrue. But she didn't have the faintest idea how to convince him of the truth. All she could do was let him walk away. And hope that she'd be able to work out a compromise that would suit them both.

CHAPTER FOURTEEN

JUST to underline his point, Dante distanced himself slightly over the next few days. But then Carenza—who'd thrown herself into work, in the hope that her subconscious would come up with a fix for the situation between her and Dante and she could find a way of proving to him that he wasn't his father—was digging through the boxes of invoices when she discovered something she really wasn't happy about. Two phone calls to check certain details made her even less happy.

She really couldn't discuss this with her grandfather, and Emilio Mancuso was the last person she wanted to know about what she'd just found out until she'd decided what to do. The only person she could really talk to about this was Dante.

It wasn't one of their mentoring days. But, right now, she really needed his help.

She picked up the phone and dialled his number.

'Mariella Ricci.'

Oh, no. His phone was through to his secretary—so the chances were, he wasn't in. 'Hi, Mariella. It's Carenza. Can I speak to Dante, please?'

'Sorry, *cara*. He's in meetings all day. Is it something urgent?'

'It's OK. It can wait.'

'You don't sound so sure.' Mariella's voice was gentle.

'No, it's fine. Just some things that don't add up and I wanted his advice.' On how she was going to deal with this. What to do for the best.

'Do you have anything you can email over to him?'

'I could scan in the papers and email them over.' Putting her suspicions down on paper might help crystallise her thoughts and she'd work out what to do for the best.

'Do that. He'll check in with me later, so I'll make sure he knows about it.'

'Thank you, Mariella. I appreciate it.'

'Prego.'

Carenza sighed as she hung up. She was about to start scanning the documents when she realised how big the file would be by the time she'd finished; it'd take ages to download and be a nuisance for Dante. Perhaps she could drop the papers in to his office instead.

And see him.

Ha. How pathetic was she?

All the same, she took colour photocopies of the invoices, numbered them all, and composed a seriously businesslike note. Just so Dante didn't think this was simply a pathetic excuse to contact him.

#1, Invoice from dairy supplier. Sent me their copy instead of customer copy. Quantity and price both lower than on customer copy. Rang them and pretended to be dippy new secretary. They faxed me more—#2–7. Note the invoice dates and numbers are the same, but the unit costs and quantities are different.

Note also who signed them.

Mancuso. And it made her blood boil, the lying, cheating, smarmy...

Ditto invoices from fruit supplier, #8–12.

Her blood pressure went a notch higher.

Nonno pays everything in cash, so the person who signed must be pocketing the difference between what the supplier charges and what we actually pay. Embezzlement? Fraud?

And then came the kicker. What she could actually do about it. If she involved the police, then her grandfather would have to know about it, and the shock of Mancuso's betrayal could cause him to have more chest pains—a full-blown heart attack, even. Nonno could die. And no way did she want to lose him—she'd already lost more than enough people in her life.

On the other hand, she couldn't let this carry on unchecked. It was the reason why Tonielli's was failing—and she owed it to her staff to be fair, to fix this. To make things right.

Maybe Dante would have a bright idea about how she could do it without any risk to her grandfather.

Would really appreciate talking strategies with you. Thanks—CT.

There. Completely businesslike. Signed with her initials. Just as if she weren't crazily in love with him and wanted to shake him for being so damn stubborn and refusing to listen to her.

But maybe if she could show him that she was learning from him, she could also show him that he could learn from her. That they had a real chance. Maybe.

She printed off the note, put the lot into an envelope, sealed it, and headed over to Dante's office.

Mariella looked at her and frowned. 'You've got shadows under your eyes and your face is thinner. You haven't been eating properly. Or sleeping, I'd guess.'

'I always look like this without foundation. I was busy today and just forgot to put my make-up on,' Carenza lied.

Mariella sighed. 'Dante's in the same state, you know.'

Carenza wasn't sure if that was a good or bad thing. It showed it was bothering him as much as it bothered her; but she also hated the thought that she was causing him pain. 'I'm working on it,' she said, forcing a smile to her face. Just, so far, she wasn't doing very well. Dante was the only person in her life who had ever said no to her, and she didn't have a clue how to change that because she'd never had to try before.

'I don't know when he'll get a chance to come back to you,' Mariella warned. 'It might not be until tomorrow.'

'Fair enough.' Carenza shrugged. 'I thought it was easier to drop them over than to send an enormous computer file.'

'Good idea.'

Though Carenza knew that Mariella had guessed: she'd also had a pathetic hope that Dante might just be there. 'Thanks for your help,' she said, and bolted. Before she said anything pathetic and needy.

She wasn't pathetic and needy. And, really, she shouldn't be leaning on Dante. Did she really need to ask him what to do, when her course of action was obvious? She was going to have to confront Emilio Mancuso with the proof she'd found, and ask him to leave the company.

* * *

Dante rubbed his temples. It had been a long, long day. And now he had a few moments before his next meeting. He glanced at his watch. With any luck he'd catch Mariella just before she left for the evening. He speed-dialled his office, and to his relief his secretary answered. 'Mariella, it's me. Anything important come up?'

'Carenza came in.' Mariella paused. 'She looked terrible. As if she hasn't been sleeping. Or eating properly.'

'I meant business,' he said, more rudely than he'd intended, but he didn't need a lecture about Carenza Tonielli right now.

'It *was* business. She brought some papers in—some things that she says don't add up. She wanted you to take a look at them and see what you thought, when you had a moment.'

'Did she leave a note?' Oh, now, why had he said something so stupid and needy? It shouldn't matter whether she'd left a note or not. Or how she'd signed it. He definitely wasn't going to ask that. Besides, he'd made the right decision for both of them. He'd done the fair thing.

'Everything's in a sealed envelope,' Mariella said.

Which was where he should leave it. But his mouth had other ideas, and he found himself saying, 'Can you open it and take a quick look?'

When Mariella read him the note, he whistled. No wonder Carenza had been worried. In her shoes, he would've wanted a second opinion, too. 'OK. I'll give her a call. Thanks.' He could drop in and see her later tonight, after his last meeting. All he needed to do was check when would be a good time.

But when he dialled Carenza's office number, he discovered that she wasn't there; the phone was answered by one of the girls from the shop.

'Do you know where she is or what time she's likely to be back?' Dante asked.

'I think she's gone to see Signor Mancuso.'

She'd *what*? Surely she hadn't been so hare-brained as to go and tackle the man about his fraudulent activities on her own, without back-up? 'Thank you. If you could let her know I've called,' he said, keeping his voice as polite and neutral as possible. Then he rang Carenza's mobile.

No answer.

Carenza never ignored her phone. Ever.

Prickles of unease darted down his spine.

He was supposed to be in a meeting in less than five minutes. An important meeting. Something that would have a huge effect on the franchising.

But no way could he leave Carenza alone in what could well turn into a seriously nasty situation. What the hell had she been thinking? That Mancuso would simply say, 'OK, so you caught me, I'll stop now'? It looked as if the man had been systematically taking a cut from Tonielli's, with nobody to check him; Gino's accountant was clearly either incompetent or in on the deal. And it was unlikely that Mancuso would take it well when Carenza confronted him with the evidence.

Dante raked a hand through his hair. If he rang Mancuso and she wasn't there, it would give the man enough warning to help him cover his tracks and lie his way out of it. But if she was there, then why the hell wasn't she answering her phone? Had Mancuso done something to her? His stomach turned to water at the idea of her being hurt. Carenza. So bright and sweet—and so damn *vulnerable*.

He had to go and find her. Now. There was no real choice.

His lawyer was waiting for him when he cut the connection on his phone.

'Vittorio, you'll have to do this without me,' he said. 'That, or get them to postpone—something important's come up and I have to go.'

'Rachele's all right? Your mother? Fiorella?'

Interesting that his lawyer had mentioned his sister first, Dante thought. They'd talk about that, later—but right now Carenza had to come first. 'They're fine. Sorry, I don't have time to explain. I have to go.'

The bike was going to be quicker than a taxi at this time of night. Decision made, he strode into his garage—not caring that he was wearing a business suit, because there wasn't time to change—jammed his motorcycle helmet on his head, and took off for Mancuso's office.

This would prove to Dante that she knew what she was doing, Carenza thought. He'd said that she needed to gather her evidence. She had—and from more than one source. And her instincts had been right on the money, too; she had proof now that Mancuso *had* been at the bottom of this all the way along. And hadn't Dante said that he'd rather she called with solutions than with problems?

She could do this. Prove her worth as a businesswoman.

It made her angrier and angrier as she reached the shop, but she kept a lid on her temper. Yelling was going to get her nowhere. She had to stay calm and deal with the facts. Show Emilio Mancuso that she knew what he'd done and it was going to have to stop right now.

As she walked into his office Mancuso looked up. 'I wasn't expecting to see you at this time of night.'

No, she'd just bet he wasn't. But she wasn't going to rise to the bait and protest that she worked longer hours than he did. It wasn't relevant. 'We need to talk.'

There was a mocking glint in his eye. 'Ah, so you re-alise now that you can't manage the business?'

'No,' she said. 'I can manage, all right. But there's a problem that needs sorting.'

'And you're expecting me to sort it?'

'Actually,' she said quietly, 'you *are* the problem. I know what you've been doing. You've been creaming off money through the supplier.'

'What are you talking about?'

Oh, he was good. A few weeks ago, that wide-eyed look of shock might have fooled her. But she knew how to read figures and spot trends, thanks to Dante's help. 'I have proof.'

He sneered at her. 'You know nothing.'

'Actually, I do.' She outlined exactly how he'd done it. 'And I have the paperwork to prove it.'

Mancuso folded his arms. 'You're bluffing, or you would've called the police.'

'I'm not bluffing.' She took the papers from the box file. 'It's all here. Plus the information they helpfully faxed over to me.' She stared at him unflinchingly. 'You deserve to be in jail for ripping off someone who trusted you, for putting the jobs of all your colleagues at risk just because of your own greed. But I don't want Nonno knowing how you be-trayed his trust. So here's the deal. You go now—and you tell Nonno it's because you want to set up on your own—or I take the files to the police and let them deal with you.'

'And how do I know you're going to keep your word on that?'

'Because Nonno always has, and I'm his granddaugh-ter. And a Tonielli's word *means* something.' She spread her hands. 'Your choice. Go now, without a fuss, or talk to the police.'

'You spoiled little bitch.' He stood up. 'Who the hell do you think you are, to talk to me like that?'

* * *

Dante walked in just as Mancuso's fists were clenching. 'Good evening,' he said coldly.

Both Carenza and Mancuso looked shocked to see him.

'What are you doing here?' Carenza asked.

'I got your message. And, as you didn't answer your phone, I thought you could do with some back-up.'

'I'm dealing with this,' Carenza said stiffly.

'I know.' He leaned against the doorframe. 'As I said, I'm just back-up.' He gave the older man a warning glance.

'Thank you.' She turned to Mancuso. 'And, to answer your question, who am I? Gino's granddaughter. His heir. The person who runs this business.'

Mancuso's lip curled. 'You weren't bothered about the business ten years ago.'

'I was little more than a child, then,' Carenza defended herself.

'Or five years ago, when Gino was ill,' Mancuso said accusingly.

'If I'd known he was ill,' she said quietly, 'I would've come straight back, and you know it.'

'He's leaned on me for years and years. Even before he was ill. I was there for him when Pietro died and he fell apart—*I* was the one who kept everything going. Me.' He stabbed his finger at his chest. 'I was there for him when he kept insisting that you were going to come home and take over, and it was obvious to everyone else you were too busy having a good time in London. *I was there.*' Again he stabbed his finger at his chest. 'And then you walked in and took over.'

'Don't blame me for this. It's been going on for years. You've been creaming off the profits.'

'Because I worked for them,' Emilio snarled. 'I earned them.'

'No. You stole from someone who trusted you. And

that's wrong.' She lifted her chin and looked him straight in the eye. 'Purely because you *were* there to support my grandfather, and I owe you for that, I'm not going straight to the police. As I said, I'm giving you the chance to leave now, without a fuss. And I suggest you take it.'

'Leave now?' He looked shocked.

'Take your personal things,' she said. 'And give me your keys. All of them.'

His fists bunched, and Dante thought he was going to take a swing at Carenza. 'I wouldn't do that, if I were you,' he advised coldly.

'And you're going to stop me?' Mancuso said.

It would be so, so easy for Dante to hit Mancuso, knock out the older man before he could touch Carenza. But that was who he was trying hard not to be. 'If you want to be in court on charges of assault and bodily harm as well as fraud, go right ahead,' Dante said. 'I'm sure the judge will have something to say when he finds out you hit a woman who's smaller than you and can't fight back. And so will the jury.' He shrugged. 'And if it's reported in the paper and a copy of it happens to be in the prison where you're sent...I gather prisoners don't have a lot of sympathy for men who hit women.' He certainly didn't.

'And I'd testify,' Carenza said. 'So it's your choice.'

Mancuso said nothing, but it was obvious that he knew he was beaten, because he gathered his personal belongings together and handed her the keys. 'Rot in hell,' he said savagely as he left, and slammed the door behind him, almost hard enough to shatter the glass.

'Is that all of them?' Dante asked when she checked the keys.

'I think so.'

'It might be a good idea to get the locks changed, just in case. Does he have keys to the other branches?'

'They're all here.' She bit her lip. 'I think.'

'Don't take the risk. Get the locks changed in all the shops,' he advised.

She frowned. 'What, right now?'

'He's an ex-employee with a grudge. If he has access to the shops, he could do a lot of damage. Starting with contaminating the ice cream. And if your customers get sick, that's your reputation gone.'

Her face was ashen as she registered all the possibilities of how Mancuso could damage Tonielli's.

'Sit down. I'll sort it,' he said softly. He called the locksmith while making coffee, and added several spoons of sugar to her mug.

She took a sip and pulled a face. 'Dante, I'm sorry, but this is horrible. It's too sweet.'

'Drink it,' he said, 'because you've just had a shock and sugar's good for shock.'

'In England, they normally do hot sweet tea.'

'Trust me, my coffee's better than my tea,' he said lightly—and was relieved to see her smile.

The locksmith arrived relatively quickly; Dante waited with her while the locks were changed, then drove her on the bike behind the locksmith to each shop in turn, ending up at the one under her flat.

'I think you need to tell your grandmother what's been going on—just in case Mancuso breaks his word and tells your grandfather a pack of lies,' he said.

'It'll devastate her. It's...' She sighed. 'It's almost as if he tried to worm himself into my father's place, acted like a son and looked after them. And it should've been *me* doing that, not him.'

'You've done nothing wrong. Don't blame yourself.'

'But if I'd been here...'

'He said he helped when your father was killed. You

were six. How could you have possibly taken over from your grandfather back then?'

She sighed. 'I guess you're right.'

'Of course I'm right.'

'It makes me sick to think about it. He thought he deserved a share of the business—and when Nonno didn't give it to him, he helped himself.'

'And your grandfather trusted him with the books, so there was no check on him,' Dante said.

'I don't understand why the accountant didn't pick it up.'

Dante shrugged. 'My guess is either he skimped the job, or he was in on it as well.'

'But that—that's terrible.'

'Change your accountant,' Dante advised. 'I can give you the name of mine.' He looked at her. 'Actually, I don't trust Mancuso. I'd rather you didn't stay at your flat tonight.'

'You think he'd—' her eyes widened '—do something to hurt me?'

'Probably not,' Dante said, 'because it would be all too obvious that he was behind it. He has a motive, because you've exposed his fraudulent activities.'

'But you think he might try something?'

'I don't know, Caz. Let's not take the risk. I have copies of the files; I'll download the recording I took of the conversation so we both have copies of that, too.'

She blinked. 'You recorded it?'

'On my phone, from just as I walked in. It's another layer of proof. Tonight, I think you should stay with your grandparents.'

She shook her head. 'If I do that, they'll worry.'

Dante knew what he should do: offer to let her stay at his. But having her stay with him would be way too dangerous for his peace of mind. He sighed. 'OK. Here's the deal. I'll stay at my mother's and you can stay at my flat.'

She looked at him. 'I can't expect you to put yourself out that much for me.'

He could see the question in her face: and why won't you stay with me? 'Caz. I'm trying to be honourable. There's no way you can stay with me without us ending up in bed together. And that's not fair to either of us.'

She said nothing, but bit her lip.

Ah, hell. 'Caz, I don't want to hurt you. Right now, I admit, I want to wrap my arms round you and tell you that I'll always protect you. Except...' His voice sounded as broken as he felt. 'I can't protect you against me.'

She sighed. 'This is your blind spot, Dante. How am I going to make you see that none of it's true—that you're denying both of us what we really want?' She looked him straight in the eye. 'You're not your father. If you were, you would've piled in just now and beaten Mancuso into a pulp. But you didn't. You protected me—and you did it all with words. The right way.'

He looked at her. 'The right way,' he echoed.

'You're not going to turn into your father,' she said softly. 'If you keep believing that, you're letting him ruin your future as well as your past. Think about it.'

Was she right? Had he been wrong, all these years? 'But I told you, I broke my father's arm. I pinned Niccolo to a wall and threatened to break every single bone in his body.'

'And you did it only because you were trying to protect someone who was vulnerable, to stop someone being hurt.' She paused. 'The rest of the time...have you ever really been in trouble?'

He thought about it. 'At school?' He shook his head. 'I worked hard. I've earned my keep since I was fourteen years old.' It was the only way to get out of the misery at home.

'In the holidays?'

'Your grandfather gave me a job selling ice cream from a kiosk on the seafront.'

'And then you made a business empire out of nothing.'

'He gave me good advice.'

'And you've repaid him for that. You have six restaurants. All your staff trust you and rely on you. So tell me, Dante Romano, just *how* are you like your father apart from possibly a physical resemblance?'

'I...' He couldn't answer.

'OK. Tell me something else. When you get a setback, what do you do?'

He thought about it. He didn't just give up. He didn't start drinking and then smashing things up, hurting people and taking out his frustrations on them, the way his father had. 'I analyse things. I look at what went wrong, and learn from my mistakes.'

And then it hit him. Maybe it was time he made peace with his past. Time he went after what he *really* wanted. Time he made the right choice for himself, as well as for everyone else.

'I love you, Carenza. That's the other reason why I came here tonight. I wanted to tell you.'

She frowned. 'Weren't you in an important meeting?'

She had him there. 'Yes. But you were more important. I thought you might be in trouble when you didn't answer your phone, and it scared me spitless.'

Her eyes filled with tears. 'You said it wasn't going to work between us. That we had to be strictly business.' She lifted her chin. 'And you're completely wrong.'

'I know.'

'You're *not* your father.'

'I know that, too,' he repeated, keeping his tone mild.

She didn't seem to have heard his admissions. 'And let me point out something else: you inherit half your genes from each of your parents. Half your genes are your mum's. The other half… Well, supposing half of your father was the violent side, and you inherited the non-violent side of him? So then you wouldn't have any of the violent genes at all.'

He couldn't help smiling at that. 'I don't think genetics works *quite* like that, Princess.'

She narrowed her eyes at him. 'Call me an airhead and I'll make you babble.'

He smiled. This was his Carenza. She'd just faced a tough situation, but she wasn't going to let it get her down. She was going to find something to smile about. 'I'm not sure if that's a threat or a promise.'

'Both. I think.' She dragged in a breath. 'I love you, too, Dante.'

'We're both going to have to learn to compromise,' he warned. 'But I've been thinking about it. This is going to work. And we're going for a full merger.'

'Merger?'

'Uh-huh. Your business and mine. Actually, make that an expansion. We can add in an art gallery. And we're not living above the shop or the restaurant. We're getting a proper house.'

'Merger.' She blinked, as if she couldn't quite take it in.

'Marriage,' he said.

Her eyes went wide. 'You want to marry me?'

'Yes.'

She coughed. 'You once told me that you were the one who asked the questions. Isn't that one meant to be a question, not a statement of fact?'

'I guess so.' He dropped down onto one knee. 'Carenza

Tonielli, I love you and I want to spend the rest of my life with you. Will you marry me?'

'I have conditions.'

'Conditions.' That was definitely the princess talking. He hid a smile. 'Do they involve high-end designer shoes and wedding dresses?'

She pulled a face at him. 'Much more serious than that.'

'Hit me with them.'

'After Paris. When you said it was for the best that my period started.' She bit her lip. 'It wasn't. Because that's when I realised that I want babies. *Your* babies.'

'A family. Yeah. That works for me, Princess.' And they were both going to have what they hadn't had when they grew up. The parent-child bond, in her case, and a happy home without violence, in his. 'And maybe we can have a dog. I always wanted a dog when I was a kid.'

He didn't explain why he hadn't had one, but she clearly guessed, because she stroked his face. 'You're not your father,' she said again. 'I saw you with Fiorella. You're putty in her hands. You'd do anything to protect her. And that's what you'll be like with our children. And the dog. And me.'

'Especially you. But do you have any idea how uncomfortable it is, resting on one knee?'

She spread her hands. 'I've never gone down on one knee to propose to anyone, so no.'

He rolled his eyes. 'Cut to the chase, Princess. Tell me the rest of the conditions.'

'You're *so* impatient.' She rolled her eyes. 'That was it. I want your babies.'

'That's what I want, too.' He paused. 'So do I get an answer to my question?'

'Yes.'

'Yes, what?'

She smiled. 'Yes, Dante, I'll marry you.'

He whooped, scrambled to his feet, picked her up and whirled her round. And then he sobered. 'I've done this completely the wrong way round. I should've asked your grandfather's permission, first.'

'He likes you. He'll say yes, as long as you make me happy.'

He stole a kiss. 'That's a definite.'

'We've got an awful lot to talk to my grandparents about tomorrow,' she said, biting her lip.

'And not all of it good, I know. It's going to be hard for them, accepting that they trusted someone who let them down.' He sat down, settling her on his lap. 'But we'll get through it, because we'll be together.'

'Always. And that's my business plan.'

'Seconded by me. So it's a deal?'

'It's a deal.'

'Good. And now,' Dante said, 'I vote we seal the deal properly. With a kiss.'

She laughed. 'I thought you'd never ask…'

* * * * *

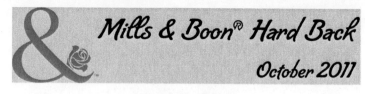

ROMANCE

The Most Coveted Prize	Penny Jordan
The Costarella Conquest	Emma Darcy
The Night that Changed Everything	Anne McAllister
Craving the Forbidden	India Grey
The Lost Wife	Maggie Cox
Heiress Behind the Headlines	Caitlin Crews
Weight of the Crown	Christina Hollis
Innocent in the Ivory Tower	Lucy Ellis
Flirting With Intent	Kelly Hunter
A Moment on the Lips	Kate Hardy
Her Italian Soldier	Rebecca Winters
The Lonesome Rancher	Patricia Thayer
Nikki and the Lone Wolf	Marion Lennox
Mardie and the City Surgeon	Marion Lennox
Bridesmaid Says, 'I Do!'	Barbara Hannay
The Princess Test	Shirley Jump
Breaking Her No-Dates Rule	Emily Forbes
Waking Up With Dr Off-Limits	Amy Andrews

HISTORICAL

The Lady Forfeits	Carole Mortimer
Valiant Soldier, Beautiful Enemy	Diane Gaston
Winning the War Hero's Heart	Mary Nichols
Hostage Bride	Anne Herries

MEDICAL ROMANCE™

Tempted by Dr Daisy	Caroline Anderson
The Fiancée He Can't Forget	Caroline Anderson
A Cotswold Christmas Bride	Joanna Neil
All She Wants For Christmas	Annie Claydon

ROMANCE

Passion and the Prince	Penny Jordan
For Duty's Sake	Lucy Monroe
Alessandro's Prize	Helen Bianchin
Mr and Mischief	Kate Hewitt
Her Desert Prince	Rebecca Winters
The Boss's Surprise Son	Teresa Carpenter
Ordinary Girl in a Tiara	Jessica Hart
Tempted by Trouble	Liz Fielding

HISTORICAL

Secret Life of a Scandalous Debutante	Bronwyn Scott
One Illicit Night	Sophia James
The Governess and the Sheikh	Marguerite Kaye
Pirate's Daughter, Rebel Wife	June Francis

MEDICAL ROMANCE™

Taming Dr Tempest	Meredith Webber
The Doctor and the Debutante	Anne Fraser
The Honourable Maverick	Alison Roberts
The Unsung Hero	Alison Roberts
St Piran's: The Fireman and Nurse Loveday	Kate Hardy
From Brooding Boss to Adoring Dad	Dianne Drake

Mills & Boon® Hard Back

November 2011

ROMANCE

The Power of Vasilii	Penny Jordan
The Real Rio D'Aquila	Sandra Marton
A Shameful Consequence	Carol Marinelli
A Dangerous Infatuation	Chantelle Shaw
Kholodov's Last Mistress	Kate Hewitt
His Christmas Acquisition	Cathy Williams
The Argentine's Price	Maisey Yates
Captive but Forbidden	Lynn Raye Harris
On the First Night of Christmas...	Heidi Rice
The Power and the Glory	Kimberly Lang
How a Cowboy Stole Her Heart	Donna Alward
Tall, Dark, Texas Ranger	Patricia Thayer
The Secretary's Secret	Michelle Douglas
Rodeo Daddy	Soraya Lane
The Boy is Back in Town	Nina Harrington
Confessions of a Girl-Next-Door	Jackie Braun
Mistletoe, Midwife...Miracle Baby	Anne Fraser
Dynamite Doc or Christmas Dad?	Marion Lennox

HISTORICAL

The Lady Confesses	Carole Mortimer
The Dangerous Lord Darrington	Sarah Mallory
The Unconventional Maiden	June Francis
Her Battle-Scarred Knight	Meriel Fuller

MEDICAL ROMANCE™

The Child Who Rescued Christmas	Jessica Matthews
Firefighter With A Frozen Heart	Dianne Drake
How to Save a Marriage in a Million	Leonie Knight
Swallowbrook's Winter Bride	Abigail Gordon

Mills & Boon® Large Print
November 2011

ROMANCE

The Marriage Betrayal	Lynne Graham
The Ice Prince	Sandra Marton
Doukakis's Apprentice	Sarah Morgan
Surrender to the Past	Carole Mortimer
Her Outback Commander	Margaret Way
A Kiss to Seal the Deal	Nikki Logan
Baby on the Ranch	Susan Meier
Girl in a Vintage Dress	Nicola Marsh

HISTORICAL

Lady Drusilla's Road to Ruin	Christine Merrill
Glory and the Rake	Deborah Simmons
To Marry a Matchmaker	Michelle Styles
The Mercenary's Bride	Terri Brisbin

MEDICAL ROMANCE™

Her Little Secret	Carol Marinelli
The Doctor's Damsel in Distress	Janice Lynn
The Taming of Dr Alex Draycott	Joanna Neil
The Man Behind the Badge	Sharon Archer
St Piran's: Tiny Miracle Twins	Maggie Kingsley
Maverick in the ER	Jessica Matthews